DATE			

KINGFISHER
a Houghton Mifflin Company imprint
222 Berkeley Street
Boston, Massachusetts 02116
www.houghtonmifflinbooks.com

First published in 2007
2 4 6 8 10 9 7 5 3 1

LIBRARY OF CONGRESS CATALOGING-IN-PUBLICATION DATA
has been applied for.

ISBN: 978-0-7534-5896-9

Printed in India
1TR/0107/THOM/SCHOY/60BNWP/C

Recipe for Rebellion

Cathy Hopkins

KINGFISHER
BOSTON

Chapter One
Bat poop

"Danu Harvey Jones. Can you read us the poem you've written about family?" asked Mr. Beecham, peering over his glasses at the front of the classroom. "And sit up straight."

"It's Dee, not Danu," I said.

"I think not, Miss Harvey Jones. We call ourselves by our proper names at this school. We don't use nicknames, and your given name is Danu. Now, stand up and read us your poem."

I stood up and took a deep breath.

"My aunt is full of bat poop,
My brother is a twit,
My parents have deserted me,
I don't know where I fit."

A few girls at the back of the class snickered as Mr. Beecham's mouth shrunk to look like a cat's bottom.

"That's enough, Danu," he said. "Sit down. I don't think we need to hear any more of that. See me after class."

I sat down. I'd probably get detention again.

I didn't care. At least there would be a few people around in there, and it would be better than going back to the empty apartment. Again.

Joele Morrison was next up reading her poem. I rolled my eyes. It was about a cute kitten playing on the grass and her ickle, lickle baby brother rolling into a flower bed. Blah. Vomitous and a half. My poem had at least told the truth about my situation, and what else was I supposed to write? About kittens and babies? Yeah, right. A kitten would die of malnutrition where I was living now, and as for an ickle, lickle baby brother, there was just no space for anyone else. In fact, there was hardly a flower bed to roll into and not a tree to be seen.

For the rest of the lesson, as my fellow classmates droned on with their pathetic poems, I gazed out the window and thought about my old life. What were my old friends doing at this moment as I sat here having to endure Death by Bad Poetry? I hated my life. I hated my new school. I hated everyone in it. My world was rotten.

It hadn't always been like this. I didn't always live in the rat hole that I do now. No. Once I had a life. A life I was very happy with, thank you very much. I lived in a town in Maine with my dad, who's an archaeologist. He's famous in some circles. My mom died when I was three, and my dad had a lady from

town come in to do our housekeeping. Mrs. Wilkins. She was lovely. Kind and happy and the most fantastic cook. There was always the smell of something wonderful baking in the oven when I got home. I attended the local school, and in fact I was able to walk there from our old house. It took ten minutes, through the back field, five minutes along the coast road, and there I was. I had lots of friends. Bernie, Fran, Annie, and Jane. I had a dog, Snowy (he was jet-black). I had a cat, Blackie (he was pure white), and I used to be able to ride our neighbor's horse. They let me name him, so I called him Spot (he was a chestnut). There were birds and squirrels in our yard. I had a huge bedroom with a bay window looking out over rolling fields and woods. I was happy.

One day, Dad was waiting for me when I came home from school. I could tell the moment I set eyes on him that something was wrong. At first I thought someone had died or something had happened to Snowy or Blackie. But no. Nothing like that. Dad had been offered a year's contract working on some ancient site in South America digging up old bones and stuff. Chance of a lifetime. The one he'd been waiting for. Etc., etc. Blah-de-blah-de-blah. And that was the end of life as I knew it. Why couldn't he go and leave me with Mrs. Wilkins, as that's what usually happened when there was a dig? I asked. But he wouldn't hear of it. Other digs had been for a weekend, two weeks at the longest. This was the big one and would take him away for a whole year. I begged to be able to stay at the house, but he'd already arranged for it to be rented out for the year. Nothing I could say or do would persuade him to let me stay. I tried to organize it so that I could live with one of my friends, but no one had any room. I'd be "just fine," said Dad. He'd arranged for me to attend a boarding school close to where his sister lived. He'd be back to see me during school vacations, and my aunt would keep an eye on me in the meantime. I was a grown-up girl. I'd soon adjust. That was the time I realized that he cared more about a bunch of old dead bones than he did about me, his living daughter.

"Danu, *Danu*," said a stern voice in my ear. It was old Beecham again. What did he want now?

"Yes, sir."

"Have you been listening to anything that is going on in this lesson?"

"Yes, sir. Kittens. Ickle babies."

Mr. Beecham sighed and then went back to the front of the room. "Class dismissed," he said.

I got up to go with the others.

"Not you, Harvey Jones. I want a word."

I slumped back down into my chair. I was very popular with the teachers at this school. They were always keeping me back for "a word."

Mr. Beecham waited as the rest of the class filed out. A few of the girls turned and stared at me and then whispered to each other. I stuck out my tongue at them.

When the others had left, Mr. Beecham came and sat at the desk across from me and looked at me with concern.

"So, Danu. How are you settling in?"

I shrugged. "Okay."

He sighed again. "And how's life at home?"

"Not at home . . ."

"Ah, yes, I meant your home now. I believe you're living with your aunt?"

I shrugged again. "Yeah."

"And are things all right there?"

"Yeah." I wasn't going to tell him the truth. There was no point. Nobody could do anything to get me out of there.

Mr. Beecham coughed. "Well, Danu . . . I'm afraid we're going to have to do something, aren't we? About your attitude."

I shifted my feet and looked out thc window.

"Have you got any suggestions?" Mr. Beecham persisted. "And please look at me when I'm talking to you."

I turned back to him. "Whatever."

"'Whatever' is not an answer. I have your records from your past school, Danu, so you don't fool me. You were a straight-A student, and now your highest grade is a D. What are you going to do about it?"

"Work harder," I muttered. I had no intention of working harder. My plan was to get expelled, and then with a bit of luck, I could go back to my old school. Even if it meant living in the dog kennel with Snowy, I wouldn't mind.

Mr. Beecham stood up. "I hope so, Danu. I hope so. We're here to help, you know, not hinder, so I'd appreciate a bit of effort on your part. And . . . I also need to talk to you about . . . well, about your hair . . ."

"What about it?" I asked. It had taken me months to get it into decent dreadlocks. Since my hair is fine and reddish blonde, it had taken weeks and weeks of twirling and twirling before the coils stayed, but at last I was starting to look the part. I'd even wound some green and pink yarn through some of them. My dreadlocks were part of my plan. I had to look like a rebel as well as act like one.

"Well . . . don't you ever comb it?"

"No way."

"But that can't be hygienic."

I shrugged. "Is there a rule that says I can't wear my hair like this?"

"Not exactly."

"So what's the problem?"

"It makes you look, well, how can I put this . . . rather unkempt."

"Do you tell other girls how to wear their hair?"

"No. I don't make a habit of it."

"Okay, then. Can I go now?"

Mr. Beecham sighed. "I suppose so."

I made my way out of the school and through the playground to the bus stop. Girls were still hanging around, chatting and laughing. I kept my head down. I wished that I had a friend here. I wished that I had someone's house where I could go to and hang out in, gossiping about the day, about other kids. But no, the only place I had to go back to was the prison of an apartment where I lived with my aunt, the warden.

She lives in a small apartment on the fifteenth floor of a tall building in a new development area. No grass, no trees, no animals, and no outside space except for a tiny balcony with one dead plant on it. Aunt Esme earns good money at her job, but she chooses to live in this no man's land because it's close to her office. Okay for her since she's never home. I felt like I was suffocating there. There's nothing to do. Nowhere to go; it's not safe out after dark because of its proximity to a rough neighborhood. I was going to end up like that poor geranium on the balcony. Dead.

I caught the bus and sat looking out at the gloomy winter's night. We'd turned the clocks back last week, so it was dark early. On the street, people were huddled in their coats, rushing to get home out of the cold. I got off at the square where Aunt Esme lives and sloped over to her building. Up the steps, through the door, into the elevator that smelled damp, like boiled cabbage, and up to her floor. It was like being in some sci-fi movie about the future, where all traces of natural life had been destroyed and all that was left was concrete.

I let myself into the apartment, turned on the lights, and went into the living room to turn on the TV. I always did that the minute I got back, as the sounds of people on TV made me feel as if I wasn't totally alone. I slumped down to watch. No point in going to the fridge. Aunt Esme didn't buy real food, only fancy assorted lettuce leaves in plastic bags. And sometimes there was a lemon in there for her gin and tonic. She never cooked at home, as she ate out most evenings with her job or grabbed something at the office, where she usually worked late.

At six o'clock precisely, there was a knock at the door. It was Rosa bringing my dinner. She works as Aunt Esme's cleaner, and when I moved in, she was hired to cook and then bring me my dinner every evening as well. She's Polish, around 20, and hardly speaks any English

She came into thc hall and pointed toward the kitchen.

"Put in microwiv?" she asked.

"No, I'll take it," I replied. "Thank you."

She handed me the dish and then left.

She wasn't a bad cook, actually, although her repertoire was somewhat limited. Some sort of goulashy thing with carrots and beans every night. *Still, better than soggy lettuce*, I thought as I heated it up and took it back to eat while I watched TV.

It was too hot, and the first forkful burned the inside of my mouth. I felt tears prick the back of my eyes.

"Bat poop," I said to the empty room.

I had never felt so alone in all of my life.

Chapter Two

Aunt Esme

"Danu, come and clean up this mess this instant," called Aunt Esme from the living room the following morning.

I was in my bedroom, e-mailing my old friends. I turned off the computer and went to face the firing squad. What did she want now?

In the living room, Aunt Esme was dressed in her usual black business suit, white shirt, dark hair pulled back in a neat bun, and she was busy dusting the shelves. She was crazy. She cleaned up after Rosa had been *and* before she came.

"What mess?" I asked. The room looked fine to me. It always did. Okay, the carpet was a bit faded, but there wasn't anything to mess up. One L-shaped cream Italian sofa still with its plastic wrapping on (in case anything got spilled on it). A faded cream carpet (Aunt Esme said that she'd get around to replacing it one day, but at the moment, she was too busy, busy, busy). White walls with no pictures. A set of bookshelves with only a Yellow Pages and a road atlas on it. A glass coffee table. One square glass vase in an empty fireplace. No flowers in it. I hated the place. She hadn't even gotten around to putting up any curtains or blinds in the windows. It was the coldest room that I'd ever set eyes on, not the kind of place you could curl up and be cozy in, but then Aunt Esme never did that. All she did was work, work, work. She's a lawyer and lives and breathes her job.

Aunt Esme pointed at the dinner plates that were still on the coffee table from last night.

"I've told you before about cleaning up after yourself. It's really not too much to ask, is it? You know I don't have time when I get back from work," she said, and glanced at her watch, "and I certainly don't have time now because I have to get to the office."

"And a good morning to you, too," I said.

"No need to be sarcastic," said Aunt Esme.

"I was going to do the dishes. Honest. Give me a break."

Aunt Esme made an effort to force a smile, but it came out more like a grimace. "So, what are you going to do with yourself today?"

"Nothing. There's nothing to do."

"Homework?"

"Done it." I hadn't, but she didn't need to know that.

"Then do you want to go and get a couple of DVDs from the store?"

"*Again*? I think I've seen everything they have there. I'd hoped that maybe we could do something. Go somewhere."

"Danu, I can't. Really. I have a major case on at the moment, and it's taking every minute I've got."

I slumped down on the sofa.

"Feet, feet," said Aunt Esme, swatting my legs off her sofa.

"I've got clean socks on," I objected. "And the sofa's covered."

"I don't care. We don't put our feet on the furniture in this house."

"Don't do this, don't do that. It's like living in a prison, there are so many rules."

Aunt Esme sighed. "My house, my rules. You knew that when you came here."

"It's not a house. It's an apartment."

"Oh, don't be difficult, Danu. You know what I meant." She glanced at her watch again. "Have you had breakfast?"

"Like you care."

Aunt Esme sighed. "Actually, I do care. Have you had something?"

"Yes. I had dried yak's ear and a slice of lemon. It was all that was in the fridge."

"Very funny. Rosa will be in this evening as usual with your dinner, but what about lunch? I'll leave you some money, and you can get yourself something."

"Whatever."

Aunt Esme put on her jacket and found her bag. "Okay, then. See you later."

I flicked on the TV. "Later."

Aunt Esme hovered for a minute. "Look, I know that I've been busy lately, and I'm sorry. Haven't you made any new friends at the school that you can see?"

"They all hate me."

"I'm sure they don't."

"Do."

Aunt Esme sighed again and rooted around in her bag for her wallet. "Look, I can't get into this now. Here's twenty dollars–get yourself some lunch. In fact, make it thirty. Take ten for some spending money. And, oh, can you get a couple of lemons while you're out?"

"Whatever . . ." *Spending money. Pfff,* I thought. *What was I going to spend that on around here*?

"And *stop* saying 'whatever.' It's driving me crazy." She picked up her bag and for a moment hovered at the door. She looked awkward. "Um . . . um. . . Danu . . . I . . . I also wanted to mention something. Um. The week after next I have to go to New York . . ."

"New York! For how long?"

"Oh, not long. Only a week."

"But . . . the week after next is not just any old week. It's my school break. What about me?"

Now Aunt Esme did look uncomfortable. "School vacation. Oh God, I didn't realize. Listen. Don't worry. I've asked Rosa if she can stay while I'm away, and she's agreed, so you won't be alone."

I crossed my arms over my stomach. "Like anyone cares."

A look of exasperation flashed across Aunt Esme's face. "What else can I do, Danu? It's part of my job. I've always had to travel from time to time, and I told your father that before you came here."

"He doesn't care either," I said. "Go to New York. I don't care at all. In fact, I hate you. And Dad. I hate everyone."

"We'll talk about it later," said Aunt Esme, and she was out the door in a flash, leaving me alone once again. *Huh*, I thought, *go to New York. It's not as if we spend any time together when you're here. I don't care. I won't care*. I gazed at the TV. *Saturday morning cartoons. My new friend*, I thought as I flicked through the channels. *My only friend.* I never used to watch TV in Dorset on the weekends. I had too many things to do. Places to go. Things to do with Bernie, Jane, Annie, and Fran. A ride on Spot. A walk with Snowy. I hoped that Snowy and Blackie were all right with their new owners. The family that had taken over our old house had children and they loved pets, so it was decided that ours would stay so that they didn't get disrupted. Huh. Not that I begrudged them for being allowed to stay since I wanted them to be happy, but it seemed that even the animals' feelings were taken into consideration more than mine.

I watched TV for an hour or so and then did a bit of homework. E-mailed my friends again. Then sat and stared at a wall. I remembered seeing a movie once where the woman in it talked to the wall in her kitchen. *Shirley Valentine*, that's what it was called. I thought that she was crazy at the time, but now, I could totally relate.

"Okay, wall, what should I do today?"

It didn't reply. I didn't think that it would. That really would be crazy I got up to look out the window. Another gray November day. Still not raining at least. I never used to mind the onset of winter in the country since each new season brought new colors and new scents. Back home, the leaves would be just coming down from the trees, covering the fields in carpets of glorious reds, oranges, and yellows. The air would be crisp and cold and would smell of burning leaves. Here, there was only gray cement. No color at all. And the only smell was from rotten food in the garbage cans around the back of the apartment building.

Maybe I'll go and take a walk down to the store, I thought as I stared out. *Buy some macaroni and cheese or something really exciting like that.*

I grabbed my coat and scarf and made my way out of the building, through the square, and over to the store that is run by Mr. Patel, where I bought a loaf of bread and ramen noodles and then looked at the DVDs at the back of the store in the hope that he had something new. But no. I'd seen them all.

As I was walking back across the square again, I noticed that a small crowd had gathered close to the abstract, round sculpture in the middle. *What are they watching?* I wondered. Nothing ever happened around here. Surely they couldn't be admiring the sculpture–it was only an enormous, round granite ball. Not worth looking at, really.

I joined the group and stood on tiptoe to try and see over their shoulders. Mrs. Patel, the store owner's wife, saw me and moved to her left so that I could see better. She was there with her daughter, Sushila, who glanced at me and smiled in acknowledgment. I knew her vaguely since she went to the same school as me, and we often caught the same bus. But we'd never spoken because she always seemed to be surrounded by her friends.

In the middle of the crowd was a street performer balancing on a unicycle. He (or, at least, I thought that he was a he. He had such delicate features that he could have been a she) looked like he was in his early twenties and was dressed in an electric-blue bodysuit with a silver lightning streak painted across his face. *Definitely a he,* I decided as I took in the slim, flat-chested body and long legs. He was moving in clockwise circles and juggling balls. He looked wonderful–a blast of color against the gray sky and buildings. I stood and watched for a while, and then when it was over, he started to hand out leaflets. *Some business promotion*, I assumed and began to walk away.

"Hey, you. Gloomy girl!" called the juggler.

I turned back to see the man approaching me. *What nerve*, I thought, *calling me gloomy. What did he know?*

"Surprise," he said. With a flourish, he handed me a leaflet.

I glanced at it. It seemed to be advertising a café of some kind.

"Yeah, right," I said. "Big surprise. What are you selling exactly?"

"Not selling. Just letting you know."

"Know what?"

"About Europa."

"Which is . . ."

"A deli," he said, and grinned. "The best in the area."

"A deli? Around here? Now that *is* a surprise. You're kidding."

"No, I'm not. Expect the unexpected. You should go. Cheer you up. It's good."

I hate people who tell me to cheer up, so I gave him a withering look, but he grinned back at me. I glanced down at the leaflet again. It was covered in planets and stars, and a menu was printed on the back. *Maybe I should go*, I thought. The dishes listed looked a lot more appetizing than the ramen noodles I had in my shopping bag.

"Okay, then. Where is it?" I asked. "I've never seen a deli–in fact, I've hardly seen any stores."

The juggler looked at me and sighed and then said very slowly as if I was stupid, "So . . . travel. Take . . . a . . . bus . . ."

"Which bus?"

The man pointed toward the bus stop. "Number seventy-three. Takes you right there."

The 73 is my bus to school. I'd never noticed a town on the way, so maybe it was in the other direction.

Mrs. Patel nodded her head. "He's right. The seventy-three takes you right into Osbury. Very popular place. Nice town."

Popular place. Nice town. How come Aunt Esme had never told me about this place? Then again, she never went anywhere locally. Only ever took her train into the city, returning again late at night. She'd probably never even been to Osbury.

"I'm going in with Sushila on the next bus," said Mrs. Patel. "And I know that café and the owner. You want to come with us?"

I considered my options. The empty apartment, TV, and ramen noodles. More history homework. Or a trip to discover a town where there was a deli selling tantalizing-sounding meals. And Aunt Esme had said get yourself some lunch. There might even be some interesting stores nearby to hang around in and kill some time.

"Whatever." I shrugged and followed Mrs. Patel to the bus stop.

"Whatever," said the juggler, mimicking my voice and getting off his unicycle to wearily slope after me like he was my shadow. My shadow with rounded shoulders. Mrs. Patel laughed, but I wanted to sock him. I didn't look or sound *that* bad, and I certainly didn't walk with such round shoulders. As we stood waiting for the bus, he gave us a wave and then went off to gather his things from the middle of the square. When the bus arrived, my last glimpse of him was on his unicycle, a bright blue umbrella in one hand, riding in circles around the sculpture.

Chapter Three
Joe

The bus wove its way through street after boring street: past new houses and high-rise apartment buildings similar to Aunt Esme's, with paved squares, past our school, through another subdivision. I couldn't imagine a town in the middle of all this. It was a concrete jungle. Gray and heartless. Then, suddenly, there was a field. And another one. The view was opening up. Trees! Space. Color. Leaves in soft yellows, vivid oranges, deep reds. Fields of grass, green and yellow from the summer sun. Even the clouds seemed to be giving way to a clear blue winter sky. I began to feel like I could breathe again.

"Not far now," said Mrs. Patel from the seat in front of me.

"I never imagined that we were so close to the country."

Sushila looked at me as if I was crazy, so I went back to gazing out the window. Past an old lodge called Chiron House, then a huge wrought-iron gate that had the name "Avebury" on it. *Oh. So that's where it is*, I thought. That was the school that I was supposed to have gone to. A private boarding school. Dad had filled in all of the applications, put them somewhere safe, and then had forgotten to send them off. Typical. My dad might be considered in some circles to be one of the best brains, but he was hopeless when it came to organizing anything. Ditzy when it came to anything domestic. By the time he realized that he'd neglected to send off the application, all of the places at Avebury had been taken. Not that I wanted to go there at the time, but it might have been better than where I ended up. At least at Avebury all of the students were boarders, and I would have had company.

There was an almighty last-minute panic when Dad had realized his mistake–like, what are we going to do with Danu? Dad's flights had been booked. Everything was arranged. For him. Frantic phone calls were made. He even considered sending me to to be close to my brother Luke, who's at college, but that was soon vetoed since Luke lives in a student dorm, and Dad feared that I'd be led into evil studenty ways and turn into a drug addict or a psychopath. Aunt Esme was our last option, and she wasn't too pleased with the idea of having me live with her full-time. That wasn't part of her plan. If I'd gone to Avebury, I'd only have had to stay with her

during Christmas, Easter, and in the summer. Dad did his groveling act to talk her into it, saying that she was going to have had me during vacations anyway. In the end, she gave in. She even found me a place in the local school. If it had been left to Dad, I might have ended up living with Aunt Esme and attending school a million miles away.

"Our stop," said Mrs. Patel as the bus made a turn and then drove down a street that was lined on both sides with stores and cafés. At one end, I could see an old church with a steeple, a church hall, and a small park in front. At the other end of the street was a bus stop, a phone booth, and mailbox.

"Excellent," I said, rising to get off with the Patels when the bus stopped. A place to explore. I couldn't wait.

"I'm getting the bus back at four o'clock," said Mrs. Patel. "You can come back with me if you would like or later with Sushila."

Sushila didn't say anything. She saw a bunch of her friends hanging out by the bus stop and took off with a brief "Later" to her mom.

"Thank you, Mrs. Patel," I said. "I'd like that." I can be polite if I want to be, and I even smiled, which is something I hadn't done for weeks.

Mrs. Patel took off toward a florist, so I stood at the bus stop and tried to decide where to go first.

I felt like a kid at Christmas who thought that she hadn't gotten any presents and then discovers a Santaland full of them. Osbury looked like a cute town, reminiscent of home. As I strolled along to the left, I spotted Europa, the deli. *I won't go there yet,* I thought. *I'll save it for later.* Next to the deli was a beauty salon called Pentangle. Across the street was an optician, a drugstore, and a mini supermarket. *Plenty to look at,* I thought as I passed a tanning salon, a couple of clothing stores, an interior design shop, a fish-and-chips restaurant, and a party and magic store with what looked like an Internet café at the back. A magic store? I peered in through the window. To my amazement, I could see the juggler who'd been in the square earlier! He was helping a customer from behind the counter. He looked up and gave me a wave. *How did he get back here so fast?* I wondered. He wasn't on the bus with us. He beckoned me to go in.

I didn't hesitate since his store window looked interesting, with a lot of stuff that would come in handy for the next stage of my plan to get kicked out of school. I decided to go in and take a closer look.

"Hi, gloomy girl," said the juggler as soon as I walked in.

"My name is Danu, actually," I said as I glanced around. "*Not* gloomy girl. But you can call me Dee."

The inside of the store was futuristic in style with

a lot of top-of-the-range computers in the back area, where a couple of customers appeared to be surfing the Internet. The front of the shop was painted electric blue with silver flashes across the ceiling, not unlike the juggler's costume and face paint.

"Danu. How fabulous. Oh, you can't shorten it to Dee. It's the name of a goddess."

"Wow!" I said with genuine amazement. "You're the first person I've ever met who knows that, besides my family."

"Oh, I think you'll find that a lot of people here in Osbury know their gods and goddesses. My name is Uri," said the juggler as he leaned over the counter to shake my hand. I took his hand to shake it back, and a loud buzzer went off, giving me an electric shock. It didn't hurt, but I wasn't expecting it and almost leaped out of my skin.

"Perfect," I said. "Can I buy one of those?"

Uri grinned. "You can indeed. Planning to surprise someone?"

"A few someones, actually. What else have you got?"

"What haven't we got?" asked Uri, who then proceeded to show me half the contents of his store: itching powder, blood capsules, fake dog poop, soap that makes your face dirty, a remote control fart machine, an exploding pen . . . There were all sorts of wonderful practical jokes and tricks, and I left half an hour later with a shopping bag full of purchases to try out at school next week.

After the magic store, I went into a couple of clothing stores and tried on a few T-shirts. I browsed in a bookstore and began to enjoy myself for the first time in weeks. It certainly beat how I'd spent the last few weekends—on my own, having one-sided conversations with walls.

After wandering around for a while, I began to feel hungry. Someone walked past me with a bag of fries, and the alluring smell of salt and ketchup made me realize that it was time for lunch. I looked around for a restaurant and soon spied a likely place across the street. The door was painted with a picture of a bearded man with a trident in one hand and a fish in the other. The shop was called Poseidon. *That must be fish and chips*, I thought as I crossed the street. The door clinked open, and inside I could see a man with a white beard, not unlike the man in the painting on the door. He was serving a customer. When he'd finished, he turned to me and did a double take.

"Oh. It's you," he said as if he was unhappy to see me.

I looked around. I didn't know him, so why had he said, "*Oh. It's you,*" like we'd met before and he didn't want to see me?

“Um, fish and chips, please.”

The man pulled a silver cover down over the food. “Sorry. We’re closed,” he said. “Try the deli.”

“But . . .” I’d seen that there was lots of food left. Why was he turning me away? “But there’s some left.”

“Lunch break,” he said. “Closed.”

I felt my mouth watering. “Please, can’t you just serve me and then close for lunch? I’m starving.”

The man shook his head. “Closed. Try the deli.” He came out from behind the counter and went to the door, where he pulled down a blind. “Off you go.”

Mean man, I thought as I went back out into the street. I felt hurt by his rejection. It was so totally what I didn’t need at this stage in my life. *Maybe this town isn’t so nice after all*, I thought as I bit back sudden tears.

I made my way to the deli and peered in the window. It looked cozy in there. *Should I risk being rejected again?* I asked myself. *Maybe the people in there are mean as well.* My stomach’s rumbling gave me my answer. *I’d better get in fast*, I thought, *in case they want to close for lunch, too.* I opened the door to see that there were about eight wooden tables, most of which were occupied with customers digging into large, steaming plates of food. The smell of garlic and onions filled the air, and my mouth started watering again. I felt as if I hadn't had a real meal in ages.

At the back of the deli was a big, jolly-looking man with a round belly who was slicing tomatoes. He was wearing a navy apron printed with the planets and stars–the same design that was on his leaflet. When he saw me, his rosy face broke into a huge grin.

"Hey. *There* you are," he said, coming toward me with his arms open in a welcoming gesture. For a moment, I thought that he was going to hug me, so I took a step back and turned around to make sure that he wasn't looking at someone else. But no, it was definitely me. *What is it with this town?* I wondered. *Everyone seems to think they know me. At least this guy looks friendly, unlike his fishy neighbor.*

"Um. Yes. Here I am. You are open for lunch, aren't you?"

"What does it look like?" the man said with a smile as he ushered me to a table in the corner and then thrust a menu into my hand. "You look hungry. What would you like?"

I glanced over the menu. It all sounded wonderful. Some Greek dishes, some Italian.

"I'm Joe," said the chubby man. "Joe Joeve. Now, let me get you something to drink while you choose."

I watched him go back to the counter, smiling and beaming at everyone. Clearly he was like this with all of his customers, greeting everyone like they were a long-lost friend. I wasn't going to object. I could use a long-lost friend at the moment.

Two minutes later, he was back with a big mug of what looked like hot chocolate. "Made with real chocolate," he said as he placed it in front of me. "And melted marshmallows. So, what will it be?"

"Um, today's special, please."

"One lasagna special coming up," he said with another big smile, and he was off again.

As I sat waiting for my lunch, I glanced at a small shelf to my left. It was full of books. Travel books, I noticed. To the right of my table was a bulletin board. There was a jumble of leaflets announcing local events pinned up there. Festivals, book fairs, garage sales, birthday cake makers, people offering to walk your dog, babysitters, bikes for sale, a man who could fix lawn mowers.

I felt a wave of sadness come over me. This town—and especially the café—reminded me of all that I'd left behind. A sense of community. Familiarity. Belonging. I'd taken it all for granted at the time. Back home, I'd walk through our town, and everyone would either stop to stroke Snowy or ask about my dad. I knew all of the store owners and their families. I'd known them all my life. And there was always something going on. A concert at Christmas. Bake sales at Easter. Festivals in the summer. Trick-or-treating at Halloween. Fireworks on the Fourth of July. Living at Aunt Esme's felt like living in a wasteland. People didn't know or talk to their neighbors. People were careful not to make eye contact. I knew no one besides the Patels, and I only knew them because I shopped at their store.

I got out my phone and scrolled through for Dad's number. He'd said that I could call him any time, anywhere. I pressed his number and waited. As usual, his phone was on voice mail. Dad hadn't quite joined this century as far as cell phones. He got the concept that it was a phone that you could take anywhere, but he hadn't quite grasped the fact that you had to keep it turned *on* and the battery charged. I was always having to recharge his for him when he was home. Without me there to remind him, he'd probably let it go dead.

I decided to leave a message in the hope that he'd remember to pick up his voice messages or charge his battery sometime. Somehow, I doubted it, though. He could decipher ancient alphabets and translate almost extinct languages, but the chances of him picking up a message in this century from a live person were next to none.

"Hi, Dad," I said. "I want to beg you one last time–please, please, please can I go home and back to my old school. It's not working here. I hate it. I've never been so miserable. I know I'm not quite thirteen and you're mainly interested in things that are at least two thousand, but please listen. Everyone hates me. I don't belong . . ." Suddenly, I jumped. Joe was standing to the side of me, and it seemed like he might have heard me, so I turned off the phone. He was looking at me with the saddest expression. "Oh dear," he said with a shake of his head. "Oh dear, oh dear, oh dear."

I felt myself start to blush. Was he mocking me? I wasn't sure. I gave him my best "I don't care" look and tried to pretend that I hadn't been begging my dad to let me go home a minute earlier.

"Is that my lunch?" I asked in my best grown-up voice.

Joe nodded. He sat down across from me and put a steaming plate in front of me. It smelled wonderful, of tomatoes and cheese.

"I'm so sorry to hear that you've been miserable," he said. "Is best when everyone is happy. And *I* don't hate you. Not everybody hates you. Perhaps . . ."

"That was a private phone call," I said again in my grown-up voice.

Joe got up. "Of course. None of my business. So eat. Enjoy. Tomorrow may be better."

I kept my head down and began eating. It was the most delicious food I'd had in ages. Even better than

Mrs. Wilkins used to cook, and she was good. Joe was still standing there watching me.

I glanced up at him. "What?"

"I meant it when I said that tomorrow may be better. Life, the universe, your experience of it," said Joe. "Everything changes. Nothing lasts forever. Things will get better."

"Whatever," I said.

"Whatever," he said, and smiled back.

With that, he went over to his counter and then came back with what looked like another leaflet for the deli, because it was covered in the same planets and stars.

"Got one," I said through a mouthful of food.

"No," said Joe, looking down. "When?"

"Um, juggler this morning in the square where I live."

"You mean Uri from the magic store. No. That leaflet was for my café, to bring you here. No, this is different. Look again." He pushed the leaflet back in front of me.

This time I had a closer look. It was for a website. Something to do with astrology.

"Check it out," said Joe. "It will be good for you. Make you happier."

"Mmff," I said as I finished my lunch. I wanted to be left alone. I didn't want anyone sitting too close in case I cracked in front of them and they saw that I wasn't tough, without a care in the world. I wasn't as grown-up as I acted. Inside I was lost and sad and lonely. "I will, I will." I was interested in astrology. Back home Fran, Annie, Jane, Bernie, and I used to read our horoscopes regularly, and it wouldn't do any harm to check out what the stars had in store for me here in my new life.

"You make sure you do," said Joe, and then he began to sing. "Nobody loves me. Everybody hates me. I think I'll go and eat worms. Big ones, fat ones, short ones, thin ones, see how the little one squirms."

I almost laughed.

Chapter Four

Site for sore eyes

As soon as I got back to the apartment in the early evening, I went into my routine.

Turned on the lights. "Let there be light. Ta-daah."

Turned on the TV. "Let there be sound. Ta-daah."

Checked the answering machine. "Let there be messages for me from friends in the great big world."

There was one: "Hi, Danu. Esme here. Look, sorry about this morning. Hope you haven't been sitting in the apartment on your own. Be back as soon as I can. Oh, got to go, other line's ringing . . ."

I felt bad that I'd given her such a hard time earlier, especially since I'd had such a good day. She's not so bad really, and she had taken me in at the last moment. It can't have been easy having a teenage girl move into your personal space.

Checked my e-mails: In-box: 4.

One from Fran:

Whassup, wombat. Hope you're hanging well. Not a lot to report. School muchos dulloss. New teacher for anglaise who is megaallergic and keeps sneezing. Don't think she's going to last long. Asnuh, asnuh, achooo. Miss you missmostmuch.

One from Bernie:

Hi, Dee hi, hi dee hoh. Um. Don't know what to write today. Got a zit on my chin. Put toothpaste on it. Stings a bit. Um. That's all.

One from Jane:

Come home now. All is forgiven, and we miss you. I so wish we could find somewhere for you to stay. If I killed my brother, you could have his bed, but he refuses to drink the poison.

One from Annie:

Hey, Dee. What's happening in your neck of the woods? Hope you've settled in some more because you sounded majorly down last week, and I hate to think of you being lonely. Stay in touch. And hopefully we can come visit, or you can come here. Been keeping an eye on Spot, and he looks fine. Rosie Peters from school has been riding him, so he's okay and getting exercise. And I dropped in to see Snowy and Blackie, and they're both A-okay. I also saw Mrs. Wilkins in town yesterday, and she said to pass on her love. Wish you were still here. It's weird without you. Lots of love.

They've been good friends and made a real effort to keep in touch because they all knew that one of my biggest fears was that we'd drift apart because of the distance. I don't believe the saying that goes "absence makes the heart grow fonder." I think that absence makes the heart forget. Like Dad does about me when he goes off on one of his digs.

I was about to close down the computer when I remembered what Joe had said about trying his website. He was a kind old soul, if a bit crazy, but then I liked crazy people usually–they made life more interesting. I found my jacket and rooted around in the pocket for the leaflet and then took it back to my desk. I logged onto the Internet and typed in the address.

It took a moment for the site to upload, and slowly the screen began to fill with the image of a night sky full of stars and planets. Soft, spacey music began to play.

As I waited, I decided that I'd find my horoscope, (Sagittarius) and maybe the other girls (Fran/Taurus, Bernie/Cancer, Annie/Virgo, Jane/Capricorn) and send them theirs as a surprise. Fran would like that because she's really into astrology.

I looked for the list of the 12 signs that are usually on astrology websites, but there was only a form to fill in. *Ah, well, why not?* I thought. I'd had a good day after having met Uri. Why not see where this led as well? I began to type in my details.

Name: Danu Norwan Harvey Jones.

My dad chose my names. Danu after a West

European goddess. It means great mother. Norwan is a Northern American goddess, and the name means dancing porcupine. Annie, Jane, Fran, and Bernie are the only other people in the whole world who know the origin and meaning of my names, and they were sworn to secrecy in a ceremony performed when we were nine years old. We each put our biggest secrets on a piece of paper in a box and buried it in a secret place in the woods close to our old house. That day it was decided that from thence on, I should be called Dee, but no one remembers to call me that besides them. Not even Dad or Luke, and I've told them a million times.

Birth date and place: December 18th, Dorset, Maine.

Time: 7:45 P.M. Luckily I knew my time of birth because my dad told me that he thought that I was very considerate being born when I was. I was born at home, and there was a show he wanted to watch about Egyptian mummies on the TV at 8:00 P.M., and he was worried that he was going to miss it because Mom was still in labor. Then out I popped, just in time for him to make Mom, himself, and the midwife some herbal tea and settle down to watch his show (even then he was more concerned with old bones than new).

As soon as I'd completed the form on the screen, it swirled away as if it was evaporating. Then suddenly the computer screen began to flash on and off like a strobe at a disco. I thought that something was wrong and it was going to blow up or crash, but the screen soon cleared and up came the words "CONGRATULATIONS" in red and gold accompanied by a drumroll crescendo and a blast of trumpets.

The words "YOU ARE THIS MONTH'S ZODIAC GIRL!!!!!!!" flashed across the screen. I chuckled to myself. *Hey, Joe, do you think we're all stupid out here?* I thought. This month's Zodiac Girl? Yeah, right. Me and a million others. Doh! I'm a Sagittarius. Anyone born from November 23rd to December 21st is this month's Zodiac Girl. No big deal. Someone must have persuaded Joe to use astrology as a promotion for his business. Maybe one day, I'd stop by the deli and tell him that the site only stated the obvious. *Shame that was all there was*, I thought as I turned off the computer and went to do some homework before Rosa arrived with my dinner.

Just as I was settling down to watch TV, I heard a knock at the door.

"Won't be a sec, Rosa," I called out, thinking that she was early with my dinner tonight.

I went to open the door and found Sushila standing there. She thrust a padded envelope at me.

"You left your phone in the café in Osbury," she said. "Joe asked me to give it back to you."

"Oh! I never even realized," I said as I took the package, although I could have sworn that I had it with me when I left the deli. "Um . . . thanks."

I was about to close the door, but she was still standing there.

"Sorry. Was there something else?" I asked.

"Not very friendly, are you?" she asked.

I shrugged. I'd learned that it was best to stay neutral in my new life. No expectations, no disappointments. I was a new girl in a school where all of the friendships had already been established. I'd learned to keep my head down, to keep myself to myself. That way, I wasn't let down.

Sushila was still standing there. "So . . . gonna invite me in?"

"In? Um . . . yeah. If you want."

"Great," said Sushila, stepping inside. "I've always wanted to see in one of these apartments."

I led her through to the living room, where she took in the sparse decor.

"Wow," she said. "You only just moved here?"

"I've only been here a little while," I explained. "It's my aunt Esme's place. She's lived here for a few years, but she uses it like a hotel."

"A few years? Really? You wouldn't think so. It feels like it's brand-new. Like it's picture-perfect but unlived in."

"Exactly my sentiments," I said as Sushila nosed around a bit more and looked at the non-view out of the window.

I began to feel like a realtor showing a prospective buyer around as I led her through the rest of the apartment.

"And this, ma'am, is our small but efficient kitchen. "As you can see, all the latest appliances–microwave, fridge, dishwasher."

Sushila didn't comment; she just nodded and poked her nose into a couple of cupboards.

"Where's the food?" she asked when she saw that most of them were empty.

"Aunt Esme hardly ever eats at home," I explained and led her out of the kitchen and toward the bathroom.

"Next is the bathroom, the size of a closet, I know, but then it probably was a closet."

"Yeah, not bad," said Sushila as she took a quick peek, and then I took her into Aunt Esme's room, which, like the rest of the apartment, was painted white and had the minimum of furniture. I opened her closets to reveal rows of color-coordinated

clothes. Not that there were many colors to coordinate: black, gray, navy, beige. I couldn't resist opening her drawers, too.

"Whoa!" said Sushila when she saw the rows of neatly folded underwear. "Looks like she *irons* her underwear."

"She irons everything. That is, when she's not dusting. I think she's one of those obsessive-compulsive people. A major control freak."

Sushila went back into the hallway, so I followed her.

"My room," I said when she stuck her head in the last door.

"I gathered that," she said. "It's the only room that looks lived in. Although you haven't unpacked all your stuff."

I stepped over the boxes that she was looking at. I hadn't unpacked everything partially because there was nowhere to put things and partially because I was hoping that I wouldn't be staying too long.

"My room back home was four times the size," I said.

"So what are you doing here?"

I shrugged. "I stare at walls a lot. Watch TV . . ."

"No. I mean, what are you doing here?" She gestured around at the apartment.

"Existing. Breathing. Same as everyone else."

Sushila sighed. "I *meant*, where are your mom and dad?"

I led her back into the living room, and so she couldn't see my face, I explained on the way. "My mom died when I was three, and my dad's gone off on a job somewhere in the mountains of Peru."

"What does he do?" asked Sushila.

"Digs up old bones."

Sushila laughed. "Sounds like our dog. He does that. Bet he never thought of it as a job!"

I laughed with her. "Dad writes about them and puts them in museums."

"Cool."

"It is for him."

"Ah. You don't want to be here?"

I shook my head. "Nope."

"I'm sorry your mom died."

"So am I."

"Got any brothers or sisters anywhere?"

I nodded and almost laughed. She reminded me of myself. Always asking questions, no matter how awkward. "Luke. He's in college."

Sushila glanced at her watch. "Oops, got to go. It's my birthday today, and Mom's cooking something special. You eaten?"

I shook my head. "I have my dinner delivered."

"*Delivered?* Wow. By who?"

"My aunt's cleaner cooks for me."

"What? Every night?"

"Yeah. So?"

"You mean you can't cook yourself?"

"No. So?"

Sushila shrugged. "So nothing. So. Want to come and eat with us?"

I shook my head. "Nah. Not hungry," I said. It wasn't strictly true, but I knew that Sushila had friends, and if it was her birthday, they'd probably be there at her house, and I'd end up feeling in the way or saying something stupid and putting my foot in my mouth. "So, no, thanks."

"Whatever. Later, then . . ." She went toward the front door to leave.

I wanted to kick myself. Why hadn't I taken her up on her offer? Was I crazy? Rosa wouldn't know if I didn't eat her meal.

"Hey, Sushila," I called. "If today's your birthday, you must be a Sagittarius like me, right?"

"Yeah," said Sushila, turning back. "Half-man, half-horse, or something like that."

I nodded. "The archer with the horse's body. Yeah. That's the symbol for Sagittarius. Come and take a look at this . . . um, that is, if you've got time?"

Sushila smiled. "Sure."

I led her back into my room and turned on the

computer and went to the astrology website. I thought I'd been a bit mean turning down her offer of a meal, so in order to appear friendlier, I thought that I'd print out the page that said "Congratulations, you're this month's Zodiac Girl" when it came up.

The same night sky began to appear on the screen, accompanied by the same spacey music, and then up popped the form.

"You have to fill in your details," I said.

"Cool," said Sushila, sitting at my desk. She began to fill in her details. Date of birth, place, time.

When she'd finished, I waited for the strobe and the trumpets, but instead the screen simply cleared then gave her horoscope and birth chart. No fanfare.

"Cool. Thanks. Can I print it out?" asked Sushila.

"Yeah. Sure." I pressed the print button, and the papers began to fly out.

"You look puzzled," said Sushila. "What is it?"

"Just . . . when I did it, it kind of went crazy. Said I was this month's Zodiac Girl. I thought that it was because I'm a Sagittarius, that all Sagittariuses are Zodiac Girls because it's our month."

"So do it again," said Sushila. "See if it does it again. It might have been that you were the thousandth person to enter the site or something, and that made you a Zodiac Girl or whatever."

"Oh, yeah," I said. "I never thought of that. That's probably it."

I sat at the computer and went through the process of putting in my birth date, place and time again.

The computer began to vibrate and once again came the trumpet and drumroll. *Really* loud.

Sushila laughed. "Wahoo. Hope you don't have neighbors who like it quiet!"

"But what does it mean?" I asked.

"Dunno. You're this month's Zodiac Girl. Who knows? See if there's an e-mail address, and you can ask whoever runs the site. Whatever. Look. Sorry. Gotta go. People waiting."

I let her out of the apartment, and when I closed the door after her, I spotted the package from Joe in the hall. *Good thing that he realized that the phone was mine*, I thought as I ripped open the package. Anyone could have picked it up and taken it.

Joe had wrapped the phone in bubble wrap, and when I finally had it unwrapped, I realized that it wasn't my phone after all. He'd made a mistake. It was a beautiful phone, a deep red with an amber stone encased in it, but not mine. I went to my jacket to check if my phone was in there. I felt inside of the pocket, and there it was, where I always kept it. I'd been sure that I hadn't left it in the café, and I'd been right. *Never mind*, I thought. I could always take the red phone back to the deli one night after school and give it back to Joe.

I put it on the hall table and was about to go back into the living room to watch some TV.

Just as I put the phone down, it rang. It made me jump because it had a strange ring. In fact, hardly a ring at all. More like the trumpet fanfare that had announced that I was Zodiac Girl. At first I wasn't sure what to do. It wasn't my phone, so I let it ring. *Surely it will click into voice mail*, I thought, and sure enough, after a few moments, the fanfare died down.

Then it started again. A few decibels louder. This time there was a loud thump on the wall from next door. The phone's ring was loud enough to wake the dead.

Maybe I should pick it up, I thought. *Maybe whoever's on the other end needs to get in touch with the owner of the phone, so I should let them know that it has been misplaced in case it's an emergency. And whoever was on the end of the phone would obviously know who they were calling, so I could ask who it belonged to and could tell Joe when I handed it in. Yes*, I decided. *I'll answer the phone.*

"Hello."

"Hey, Danu," said a friendly voice.

"How . . .? Who is this?"

"Joe."

"Joe from Europa?"

"The same."

"Hey, Joe. Listen. This isn't my phone. Someone else must have left it in your café."

"No. It's yours."

"No. It isn't."

"Did you look at the site?"

"Yes."

"So you know that you're this month's Zodiac Girl?"

"Um, yeah . . . whatever that means."

"It means that this is your phone. Use it when you need help."

"Help?"

"Yes."

"From who? You mean like the police?"

"No. Help from me."

"From you? You mean like if I need a delivery? Oh, that's great. Thank you so much. I thought it was some kind of business promotion. Yeah. Thanks."

"No. That's not it at all. It's not so that you can order a delivery. I meant that you can get help from me. Joe."

"But why would I want help from you?"

"Because I'm your guardian. One month only. Special offer. Joe for Jupiter. That's me. Jupiter rules Sagittarius."

He's quite clearly deranged, I thought. *Harmless but deranged.* I decided to try and humor him. "I . . . I'm sure that's very kind, but I can't afford a guardian or whatever . . ."

Joe laughed. "No cost. Free service. Because you're this month's Zodiac Girl."

"But I already have a guardian. My aunt Esme."

"Aunt Esme. Yes. Good," said Joe. "Bring her with you one day to the deli. But, seriously, we're different sorts of guardians. Call me whenever you need help. And keep checking the site. I'll put a list of all the signs and their ruling planets on there so you can see that I'm not making it up. All of the planets are here in human form, you know."

"What?" *Definitely crazy*, I thought.

"Yeah. Human form. But enough for now. All will be revealed. And in case you try to call anyone else on the phone, you can't. Only me."

And with that, he hung up.

I went back to my computer and uploaded the site. A huge arrow appeared, pointing to a list on the right-hand side.

"Birth signs and their ruling planets," it read.

I pushed my mouse over to it and scrolled down:

Sign:	**Ruled by:**
Aries	Mars
Taurus	Venus
Gemini	Mercury
Cancer	Moon
Leo	Sun
Virgo	Mercury
Libra	Venus
Scorpio	Pluto
Sagittarius	Jupiter
Capricorn	Saturn
Aquarius	Uranus
Pisces	Neptune

Okay, right. Interesting, I thought. A list of signs and their ruling planets. But Joe had said that he *was* Jupiter and my guardian. *Was* Jupiter. And that all of the planets were here in human form. I chuckled to myself. What a loony. I'd heard of people thinking crazy stuff like they were Napoleon or a chicken or something, but I'd never come across someone thinking that they were a [illegible] before. *Wow. Respect to him,* I thought. *It's ama[illegible] being so nuts, he's managed to keep his deli going!*

Chapter Five
Nits

"Seventh grade will see the nurse first period and then sixth grade after break," Mrs. Richards announced at the school assembly.

"What's happening?" I asked Sushila as I took my place in line. I was late for school because my curiosity had gotten the better of me and I'd taken another peek at the astrology site to see if there were any messages on there for me as a Zodiac Girl. Sadly, there was nothing very exciting, only my birth chart and my horoscope, so I printed them out and had a quick look on the bus on the way to school.

Zodiac Girl's horoscope: An alignment between Uranus and Jupiter last Saturday led to surprise events.

Monday: A day for glorious rebellion—go for it.

Tuesday: The Moon moves into Cancer, causing confusion.

Jupiter is in an expansive mood and brushes your chart with possibilities, should you choose to take them.

Birth chart: Sagittarius Sun, Cancer rising, Moon in Taurus . . .

There were pages and pages. Some made a bit of sense–that Sagittariuses are known for their big mouths and for being spontaneous and sporty and that they hate being held back. They prefer roaming around outdoors and having adventures. *True, true, true*, I thought. And Cancer rising meant that I would be a homebody and that, although I might present a hard exterior, inside I was a big softy. Also true, but there were other parts of the birth chart that I didn't understand–that Saturn was square to Mars and that the Moon was conjunct with Jupiter in the third house. I don't like not understanding things, and I like a challenge, so I had tried to decipher it. This made me late getting to the bus stop, which meant that I'd gotten to school after the first bell and missed half of our principal's announcement. Not that I cared. Today could be my last day at the school if all went well, and being late was a part of my plan to get myself expelled.

"Lice," said Sushila. She took a look at my dreadlocks and then stepped back a few steps. "We all have to see the nurse. She's going to have fun with your head, isn't she?"

I rolled my eyes. "Not my idea of a fun way to start the day." But not even the school nurse could ruin the good mood I was in. I had a bag full of tricks from Uri's store to try out, and I couldn't wait to get started.

The nurse put her comb in my hair and tugged it in an attempt to drag it through.

"Ow!" I yelped, putting my hands up to grab her wrists. "You're *hurting me.*"

Nurse Torturer shook off my hands and narrowed her eyes. "Tough. It's your own fault for having this peculiar hair. It's impossible," she said as she yanked at my hair again. "I can't get the comb through. It's one big knot."

"It's not supposed to be combed," I said.

Nurse T. gave me a withering look that I think was supposed to scare me into submission, but I stared right back at her. I was thinking, I must remember that expression and practice it at home. Purse the mouth, flare the nostrils slightly, narrow the eyes, frown, and bingo! You have an excellent withering look. Nurse T.'s example was effective. She was super intimidating. Tall and bony with wiry gray hair and thin skin through which you could see the blue veins inside pulse with her blood. And she smelled of disinfectant. Not one to be messed with.

"It's not supposed to have lice, either," she said, "but unless I can get this comb through, I can't be sure whether you have them or not. So, young lady, what do you suggest?"

"That you leave me alone. Can't we leave it? I'm sure I haven't got lice."

"Not an option. I have a job to do."

"I'd know if I had lice," I said. "I'd feel them."

"Not necessarily."

"Well, even if I do have lice, I don't want you to kill them. It's cruelty to animals. I'll report you to the Humane Society. Lice killer."

Nurse T. gave me an exasperated look. "Listen, kid, I have hundreds of students to see today. So here's the deal. Either you comb out your hair, or I'll have to cut it off. The choice is yours, but I will be back to check on you–you can count on that."

"You can't make me cut my hair!"

"Try me. I'll be back next week, and either your hair is combed out so that I can get my comb through it, or it all comes off."

"I'm going to report you to the principal," I said.

"You do that," she said. "But not before I send you to see her myself.

"You do that," I said.

Great, I thought as I got up to leave. I'd love to get sent to the principal's office again. All part of the plan, and soon Dad would have no choice but to let me go back home. I couldn't wait because it was actually beginning to get boring acting tough and defiant all the time. It's not me normally. I like learning. And I like doing well in school, so it went against my norm to always be uninterested in class and not do my homework well so that I got bad grades. I didn't want it to go on too long, like months or years or anything, since I need to get good grades in the end so that I can get the job that I want. I'm still not sure what career I want, but it will be either a travel writer, a foreign ambassador, or a dancer on a music show on TV. Although you don't need mega qualifications for the last one, you do for the first two, and I didn't want to mess up my chances in the long run by this bad-girl act that I was having to pull. The sooner my plan worked, the quicker I could get back into ensuring that my school transcript was up to scratch.

When I'd finished with the lice nurse, I sneaked into the teachers' bathroom and left the dirty face soap from the magic store on one of the sinks. Then I reached up and took the mirror off its hook behind the door and hid it in the last stall. With no mirror to check their appearance, any teacher who used the soap wouldn't know that their skin had changed color until it was too late.

I made sure that I hung around by the bathroom during break so that I could see if anyone went in and used the soap. I couldn't believe my luck. A ton of teachers went in. One, two, three. First Miss Hardman went in and came out with dirty hands. I ducked around a corner, but there was no need to have worried, as she seemed preoccupied and in a rush and hadn't noticed that her hands had turned deep blue.

"What are you doing here, Jones?" Mr. Beecham asked, creeping up behind me and making me jump.

"Oh, nothing . . ."

"On your way then, on your way . . ."

He went into the bathroom and came out two minutes later with normal-colored hands. *Hmph*, I thought. *He doesn't wash his hands. Yuck.*

Next was Mrs. McPhilbin. She came from the direction of the chemistry labs and spent a good five minutes in the bathroom. *Result!* I thought when she came out with dark blue blotches all over her cheeks.

"And what, may I ask, is so amusing, Miss Jones?" she said when she saw me peeking out from behind the lockers with a big grin on my face.

"Oh, nothing," I said. "Just . . ."

A couple of sixth graders went past and stared at Mrs. McPhilbin's face and then burst out laughing. She was beginning to get worried.

"What is it? Have I got something on my face?"

"Um. Only a nose like the rest of us," I replied.

At that moment, Mr. Beecham came out of the staff room. "Good heavens, Madeleine," he said when he saw Mrs. McPhilbin. "Your face! Your *face!*"

He ushered her into the staff room, from where an anguished cry arose a few moments later. *My work is done!* I thought as I took off down the corridor. *They must have a mirror in there.*

Mr. Beecham came hurtling after me not long afterward. "Danu. *Danu.* Was that something to do with you?" he asked.

I wasn't going to deny it since it was all part of my plan to be as annoying as possible. "Yes. It is a special soap from the Black Sea. Good, huh?"

"Get to your class and see the principal at lunchtime," he said.

"Yes, sir," I said. "Thank you, sir."

He looked at me as if I was crazy, but I smiled back. Everything was working out perfectly.

On the way to math class, I took a quick detour to the swimming area. *Oh, bat poop*, I thought when I saw that there were several people in there using the pool. At the far end, in the little office, I saw Mr. Doherty, the swimming teacher, reading a newspaper. I ran over.

"Fire drill, sir," I said breathlessly. "The principal sent me over to ask you to get everyone out in the next five minutes."

"But there was no bell," said Mr. Doherty. "We would have heard it."

"There was everywhere else, sir. That's why I was sent to get you. It's clearly not working over here, but Mrs. Richards says that you should get everyone out, even if they're still in their bathing suits, and that she'll send someone afterward to see why the bell isn't working in here."

Mr. Doherty sighed heavily. "Nuisance, nuisance." He stepped outside his office and blew loudly on his whistle. "Okay, everyone. Out of the pool and into the playground. Fire drill."

A loud moan came from the swimmers, but they did what they were told and grudgingly got out of the pool, grabbed their towels, and headed out in the direction of the playground.

Five minutes later, the pool area was empty. I reached into my backpack and pulled out a bottle of dye. *Lovely*, I thought as I poured the purplish-brown liquid into the pool. It began to work immediately, slowly seeping into the water and turning it a fantastic bright red that began to spread all the way from the shallow end to the deep end. *If my old friends could see me now, they'd die*, I thought, because at my other school they used to tease me and call me Miss Goody Two Shoes. Now here I was being as bad as bad could be. And I had to admit–I was enjoying every minute of it.

My next class was math, and I'd already been in and done my "preparations" when the others were lining up for the nurse. I'd taped the sound part of my remote-control fart machine under Mr. Nash's chair.

I took my place with everyone else, and the class soon started. As soon as Mr. Nash sat down on his chair, I pressed the remote control from under my desk and a loud *thhhhhwwppppp* noise erupted from the front of the class.

Mr. Nash looked around, but, of course, there was no one behind his chair or anywhere close to it. I pressed the button again. Another *thwpppppp* blasted from his chair, and the class started laughing as Mr. Nash stood up to try and see where the noise was coming from.

I repeatedly pressed the remote control from under my desk. *Thwwwp. Thwwwp. Thwwwp.* By now, everyone in the class was laughing their heads off. It was funny, too, because, as hard as he tried, Mr. Nash couldn't figure out where the sound was coming from since there was no whoopee cushion or anything that he could actually see.

He stood at the front of the class and glared at

us. "One of you troublesome kids is responsible for this. Now, are you going to confess, or do I give all of you detention?"

By way of reply, I pressed the remote one more time. *Thwwpppp*. Everyone cracked up again.

Mr. Nash continued to glare at us, so I raised my hand.

"It was me, sir." And I demonstrated how it worked. "Great, isn't it? The man in the store said that it works from as far as fifty feet away, so we could even use it on someone in another class."

Mr. Nash sighed. "Harvey Jones. I should have known. Off with you now before I lose my temper. I don't want you in my sight for another moment. Go and see Mrs. Richards *right* now."

I saluted him. "Yes, sir. Thank you, sir. Although I already have an appointment to see her at lunchtime, I'm sure that she won't mind me dropping in on her earlier as well." I went to the classroom door and then turned back. "Maybe I should take the machine with me so that she can see how it works?"

The idea of this clearly appealed to most of the class, and a few nodded, but Mr. Nash's expression let me know that he didn't agree, so I shrugged.

"No? Okay, then, later," I said, and gave the class a little wave over my shoulder as I left.

What a great morning, I thought as I sauntered down the corridor waving through the glass partitions at anyone who could see me. I could get used to being bad.

Mrs. Richards was furious. I suppose it didn't help that I gave her my exploding pen when she couldn't find her own pen to take notes.

"The swimming pool. The soap. The . . ." she couldn't bring herself to say fart machine. "The . . . rude noise machine, the pen. What next, Danu?"

"Not sure," I said as I crossed my legs and looked thoughtful. "I've got itching powder, fake dog poop. I thought I might put that in a plate of the school lunch . . . um . . . a hand buzzer. Superglue. Fake blood capsules . . . so lots of stuff, really. What do you think?"

Mrs. Richards took some deep breaths and looked at me calmly for a few moments. I almost lost my nerve because, like Nurse Torturer, she could do an impressive scary look, but suddenly her expression softened.

"I'm not a fool, Danu," she said gently. "And neither are you. Nor are you a student known for her bad behavior, at least not until you came here. So. I take it that these activities of yours are to provoke some sort of a reaction. Am I right?"

I nodded. "Maybe."

"And what reaction would that be, exactly?"

"I think that you should give me the worst punishment there is. I think I should be expelled."

Mrs. Richards pushed the palms of her hands together and studied me over the tops of them. "Oh, you do, do you?"

I nodded. "Most definitely. My behavior has been unacceptable. Totally uncalled for."

"Unacceptable? Hmmm. Uncalled for? And if I say no?"

"I've still got my superglue, stink bombs . . ."

Mrs. Richards sat and stared at me for a good few minutes before she spoke. "Are you *threatening* me, Danu?" she finally asked.

By this point, I really was starting to feel nervous. "No. Yes. I mean . . . I just think that you should expel me."

"I think we both know that is not an option, Danu. I spoke to your father before you started here. Where do you think that you would go?"

"Back to my old school."

Mrs. Richards shook her head. "Danu, I'm sorry that your life has been disrupted. I know it must not have been easy, but this bad behavior of yours has to stop right now. Do you hear me? I'm not going to expel you. No. I'm not. But I will write to your father and let him know what's been going on. And I will see your aunt to discuss your attitude. In the meantime, you will see the school counselor. Understood? In this school, *I* set the agenda, not the students, and we don't give in to demands like yours. So you will not be getting your way. Understood?"

"Mfff," I muttered. "Understood."

I felt totally deflated. Angry that my plan hadn't worked. Frustrated that I was still going to be stuck here. And sad because it meant that I was destined to continue living in my aunt's boring, horrible apartment.

When I got back into the corridor, my phone began to play its trumpet fanfare. I answered it as fast as I could because I didn't want to get called back into Mrs. Richards' office. The screen told me that there was a text message waiting for me, so I opened up the in-box and read:

"Grant me the serenity to accept the things I cannot change, the courage to change the things I can, and the wisdom to know the difference."(by Reinhold Niebuhr)

Pffff, I thought as I glanced over it. *What would anyone with a name like Reinhold know? And anyway, I don't know anyone with that name. Some idiot must have sent the message to the wrong phone.*

Chapter Six
Bonkerooneyland

As I waited at the bus stop, I could see a few girls from school watching me and whispering behind their hands. Tales of my exploits had spread through the corridors like the flu, and I couldn't blame anyone for talking about me. I would have been discussing the fact that someone had turned the swimming pool bright red, too, if I had any friends. Which I don't.

As I stood at the bus stop trying to look cool, my zodiac cell phone began to play its strange little tune again. Any image of looking indifferent went right out the window as it blew its trumpet fanfare, and a couple of people in the line behind me snickered. *Probably a wrong number again*, I thought as I checked the in-box again. But, no, this time there was a text message from Joe.

"Hey, Danu. Zodiac Girl. Jupiter is in an expansive mood," it said. "Come for an afterschool snack!"

Not a bad idea, I thought, since I wasn't looking forward to going back to the empty apartment the way that I was feeling. Plus, I had to rethink my escape plan.

So, okay, Joe liked to think that he was a planet, so what? My friend Fran used to talk to an imaginary friend when she was little, Bernie used to have long conversations with her cat, and Annie used to think that she was a princess who had been stolen by gypsies and sold to people who pretended to be her parents. Everyone has their fantasies, and the deli was safe enough. It was a public place. It wasn't like I was doing something stupid like going to meet a stranger somewhere isolated. And I was hungry. *No better location to rethink my plan*, I decided as I crossed to the other side of the street to the bus stop for Osbury.

Joe was delighted to see me, and I was glad that I'd made the detour. Even though I'd only met him recently, I felt like I'd found a new friend, and it was nice to have a smiling face to greet me at the end of the day instead of just an empty, silent apartment.

"So, how was school today?" he asked as he placed a big mug of hot chocolate and crepes with maple syrup and bananas in front of me.

"Disaster," I said. "And I'd looked at your site this morning. It said that it was a day for being rebellious and to go for it–but it didn't get me anywhere."

"Where did you want it to get you?"

I decided to tell him the truth. I was tired of playing

the tough girl who didn't care about anything. "Home, Joe. I want to go home *really* badly. I don't belong where I am. It's horrible, and I want my old life back."

Joe sat down across from me. "Ah. Change. Nothing as certain, and nothing as uncertain."

I didn't have any idea what he meant. "Is that some kind of riddle?"

"Not really. There is nothing as certain to happen in life as change. Everything is changing, all the time. Nothing stays the same, does it? The weather, the news, the seasons, the leaves on the trees, the days of the week, every cell of your body, in fact."

"So?"

"So, sometimes the changes come from within us. We choose them, like a new hairdo or a purchase or a decision to change the decor of a room. We control them to a certain extent. Sometimes, they come from outside. We don't control them. Like an earthquake or a train accident, not our choice at all. Know what I mean?"

I nodded. "I guess. I didn't choose the change that happened in my life. That's for sure. It was decided for me."

"And that's the uncertain bit," continued Joe. "Change can make us all feel uncertain. Especially the type that we don't choose. Like, we have no control and fear what's going to happen next. But you know what?

Sometimes things change for a reason. To move us on. To help us grow and further our journey. It doesn't always feel like that at the time, I know."

"Well, I feel like my journey has gone backward. I can't possibly learn anything where I am. Nothing happens there. The only books in Aunt Esme's apartment are a telephone book and a road atlas. I love books, and my old house was full of them, in every room. And I have no one to talk to. I feel like I'm living in a vacuum. I just wish that I could be back home with things the way they used to be."

"It won't be the same there, you know. Things will have changed there, too, with your old friends, with your old town, with your old school. That will have moved on also. Nothing and nobody escapes change."

"Maybe. But at least I felt like I belonged there. People knew me and cared about me."

"You have me now," Joe said with a grin. "Guardian for a month. I will help. Help you think big!"

I didn't want to hurt his feelings, so I smiled back. "Yeah. Right. That. I guess. It's not quite the same as having my dad or Mrs. Wilkins, our old housekeeper, or my friends around, though."

Joe looked sympathetic. "I know. I know." Then his face split into a grin again. "Know what Jupiter means?"

"It's the planet of merriment and expansion, isn't it?"

I knew that because I'd looked it up at the library during my afternoon break at school.

Joe nodded. "But the word, it's from Greek *Diu Pater*. Jupiter. "God father." I'm like your godfather."

"If you say so, Joe," I said.

"Well, you don't look too pleased."

"Sorry. It's just been a hard day. Nothing turned out how I'd hoped it would, and now I feel like I'm stuck."

"Ah. But life is what you make of it, Danu. Like the saying, If life gives you lemons, make lemonade."

To Joe's bemusement, I laughed. "Actually, I *could* do that," I said. "Lemons are one of the few things that Aunt Esme actually has in her fridge! She never buys any food or cooks or does any of the normal things that make a house a home."

"Then there's a place to make a start. Make lemonade. You like lemonade?"

I nodded.

"So make some," said Joe. "This is what you have to learn, Danu, my friend. You got my text message before?"

"About coming for a snack? Yes."

"No. The one before that."

"The one from Reindeer Nebu or someone?"

"Reinhold Niebuhr. 'Grant me the serenity to accept the things I cannot change, the courage to change the things I can, and the wisdom to know the difference.'"

“I thought that was a mistake. Sent to the wrong phone.”

“No, I sent it. To make you think. Listen, Danu, if you’re not happy with the hand that fate has dealt you, then do something about it. You have two choices. Sulk or smile. Sink or swim.”

“That’s four choices . . .”

“But you know what I mean,” said Joe.

“But I *have* been trying to do something. I’ve been trying to get expelled and then I can go home.”

“Okay,” said Joe. “Let’s start there. Home. It sounds important to you.”

“Is. Was.”

“That’s because you have a lot of Cancer in your birth chart.”

“Yeah. I saw that. Cancer rising. But I thought I was a Sagittarius.”

“You are,” said Joe. “Your Sun sign is Sagittarius, but your rising sign is Cancer.”

“I don’t understand,” I said.

“There’s a lot more to astrology than being one sign. Yes, you have a Sagittarius Sun sign, but you are also affected by where the Moon was when you were born, where Venus was, Neptune, all of the planets. There are nine of them, and they all affect your birth chart in different ways. You have a strong Cancerian influence in yours. Home is very important to

Cancers, which is why you don't like being uprooted."

"Tell me about it," I said as I sipped my hot chocolate.

"Well, as a Sagittarius, you like space. It's the sign that most likes space around them, so if you're cooped up in a small apartment, it's no wonder you've been finding it difficult."

"So right. That's why I want to go back to my old house. There was plenty of space there."

"What happened to it?" asked Joe.

"Rented out to a new family."

"So you can't go back there, can you?"

I shook my head. "I guess not. But there have to be other options."

"There are *always* other options," said Joe. "Always. So, okay, let's look at them."

"Okay."

I was beginning to like Joe more and more. He was the first grown-up in ages who had actually taken me seriously. He seemed to understand why I was unhappy and was listening to what I had to say.

"So, home," he said. "Important, right? What made your house a home?"

"It was where my pets were, and they were always happy to see me when I came back from school or anywhere. There were always people around. There was always the smell of baking. It felt warm. There were books around. We had a great yard. Fresh flowers on the table. And even though Dad wasn't there a lot of the time, I knew that he was around somewhere."

"Right. Good," said Joe. "So, let's think. Which of these elements do you think that you can bring to where you are now?"

"Um. None. Not really. I can't keep my pets here. They need to go out into a yard to run around, and anyway, they have new owners now."

"What about new pets?" asked Joe.

"Still need to go out into a yard. It's not fair otherwise."

Joe nodded. "Except goldfish. You could get some fish."

"I guess. But . . . Um . . . No . . . It's really my aunt's apartment, and I somehow don't think that she'd like it. She likes the minimalist look, nothing on the walls, no decorations, no pictures, definitely no fish! The apartment smells . . . clinical somehow, like a hospital, not a cozy smell at all."

"Does she spend much time in the apartment?"

"Nope."

"Hmmm," said Joe. "Maybe she doesn't find it very cozy either. Maybe *she'd* like to see someone who's pleased to see her when she comes home. How do you greet her?"

I thought back to most of the times when she came home. Usually I was in bed asleep, or I just grunted at her from the sofa. Not an especially welcoming hello. But, then, she wasn't exactly Miss Happy-to-See-You when she came in. Usually she had something critical to say before I'd even had the chance to say hi, good morning or night, or whatever. I guess we both had a lot to learn.

"Okay. Let's go back to the basics," continued Joe. "You said something about the smell of cooking. Smells of baking. Yes. I like those, too. How about you create some of those yourself? Learn how to cook. I can give you lots of easy recipes." He got up and went to rummage around behind the counter, from where he produced a pile of papers.

"Here. Recipes. For you to try."

"*Me?* Cook? Never."

"Have you ever tried?"

"Not really."

"There you go, then. You've given up before you've even tried. So that's your choice. Loser."

"Loser? You're calling *me* a loser?"

Joe nodded. "Yeah. Loser. Given up before you've tried. The one thing you *could* change, but you, yes, *you*, have chosen not to."

"But I'm only thirteen."

"So? Where in the rule book does it say that you have to be a certain age to cook? Anyway, you're not thirteen until your *next* birthday. I've seen your chart.

You're an adventurer. You're curious. You could probably be an excellent cook. Give it a try. What's your favorite meal?"

"You mean like my death meal?"

Joe looked puzzled. "Death meal?"

"Yes. If you knew it was going to be your very last meal on earth and you didn't have to worry about calories or cholesterol or all the other stuff that adults worry about, what would it be?"

"Easy. For me, lasagna with extra cheese and homemade vanilla ice cream with raspberry sauce."

"Good choice," I said.

"But it was supposed to be *me* asking you what you liked," Joe said with a laugh. "So, what's your death meal?"

"Fries. Big, chunky ones. And ketchup to dip them in. And chocolate muffins, like Mrs. Wilkins used to make. God, I miss her cakes. She was a genius. Carrot cake. Banana. Vanilla. Almond."

"Poor Danu. No cakes. Oh, woe is me, poor, poor, little me," groaned Joe.

"Well, it hasn't been easy . . ." I began and then realized that he was teasing me.

"Hmmm," said Joe. "I am afraid that I have no sympathy at all. You could have been eating Mrs. Wilkins' cake every night if you wanted to and treating your aunt to some as well. Instead you've been moping around like a mopey moping thing. Pathetic. But . . . your choice, your choice."

"Hey! If you're my godfather, aren't you supposed to be *nicer* to me?"

"I am being nice. This *is* being nice. I'm saying that there's a lot about your life that you could change. Starting with cakes. You're too thin–you should eat more. You like nice cakes. *You* bake them. You're not stupid. What's stopping you?"

I felt a knot of rage in the pit of my stomach rise up to my throat. *You don't understand,* I thought, but then I got an image of myself as the mopey moping thing that Joe had described me as, and the feeling of anger evaporated. I couldn't think of a single reason not to do what he suggested. What he'd said had really gotten through to me. My choice. Sulk or smile. Sink or swim, and I could add another, starve or cook. Yeah. I could do that. It would give me something to do as well. Yeah. I'd even write to Mrs. Wilkins to ask for her recipes. Yes. It would be a start at least. I might even bake something for grumpy old Aunt Esme.

When Joe went over to his counter to serve a few more customers, I glanced at the recipes that he'd given me. *I might not have to write to Mrs. Wilkins,* I thought as I read through them. The ones that he'd given me seemed easy enough.

After a while Joe came back over.

"See those two over there?" he asked.

I glanced over at a man and a woman who had come in and were sitting at the window table. She was tall and glamorous with long, blonde hair, and he had the look of a young, handsome poet with a shoulder-length mane of wavy, dark hair. Both had something about them, an energy that made you want to stare at them.

"Yeah."

"Venus and Mercury. Remember what I was telling you about all the planets being here in human form?"

Oh, God, I thought. *He's gone off into Bonkerooneyland again, and just as we were getting along so nicely and I was beginning to think that he was half-sane*. I decided that it was best to humor him and go along with it.

"Okay, yes," I said. "Those two over there are Venus and Mercury?"

Joe nodded. "It's important that you understand. You have grasped that each sign has a ruling planet, haven't you?"

"Yeah." I pulled out the list he'd sent me that I'd printed out with my horoscope. "Here's the list."

"And you understand that the ruling planet is like a guardian?"

"Yeah. Godfather, *Diu Pater*, guardian," I said. "Yeah. Sort of, if you want to put it that way."

Joe's expression was serious, and he sighed. "No, Danu. I think that you are humoring me. Thinking 'crazy man.' I don't think you're really getting it."

"Not getting what?"

"That the guardians are *here*, on this planet."

I couldn't hold it in any longer, and I burst out laughing. "Sorry, sorry, Joe. But it *does* sound crazy. What you're saying is that the aliens are among us. I mean, *hello*, planet Earth to Jupiter. I think you've been watching the sci-fi channel too much."

Joe looked annoyed. "I don't watch TV. I'm telling you the truth. I told you–you have to think big, Danu."

"Okay. And how does anyone recognize these guardians, then? Do they have, like, a secret handshake?"

"Many don't ever get to meet their guardians. Only those chosen to be Zodiac Girls. And even some of them choose to ignore it."

And I can see why, I thought.

Joe looked dejected, as if I'd hurt his feelings.

"You're serious, aren't you, Joe?"

"Of course."

"And you're my guardian?"

"Yep. I've *told* you. Jupiter for Sagittarius."

"You're telling me that you're the living manifestation of the planet Jupiter and that you run a deli."

He nodded. "That's the truth, Danu."

I was determined not to laugh again since he looked so serious, and I didn't want to step on his feelings, no matter how crazy they were. He was clearly harmless and very well meaning.

"So . . . Okay. So what do the others do?"

"That's what I'm trying to tell you," said Joe. "That couple over there. She's Nessa. Manifestation of Venus. He's Hermie. Manifestation of Mercury."

"Hermie for Hermes, the messenger god?"

"That's right," said Joe. "Yep. He's my son, actually. Hermie or Mercury. The Greeks called him Hermes; others call him Mercury. He works for a company called Mercury Communications as a motorcycle messenger."

I was having a hard time holding it together. "And don't tell me–Nessa runs the fish-and-chips restaurant."

Joe guffawed loudly, causing a couple of people to look over. "No! Don't be ridiculous."

I breathed a sigh of relief. He had been teasing me. He didn't believe any of it after all.

"*Neptune* runs the fish-and-chips restaurant," Joe continued. "I think you met him briefly. Old man with the white beard? Can be a bit of a grump."

Oh, bat poop. Joe really did believe what he was saying. *Poor man,* I thought, *clearly completely bonkers.*

"Okaaaaay," I said. "So Neptune runs the fish-and-chips restaurant. Um . . . let's pick another one from the list. Here. Aquarius ruled by Uranus. So what does Uranus do?"

"Uri. You met him. Runs the magic store."

Wow, Joe may be from Bonkerooneyland, but he has a vivid imagination, I thought.

I glanced back at my list. "And Pluto rules Scorpio. So, Pluto?"

"Interior designer," replied Joe. "Stylist. Does makeovers. Transformations, that sort of thing."

"Saturn?"

"Ah, Saturn. The great taskmaster. Teaches you some major lessons in life. He's a headmaster. Dr. Cronus."

"Moon?"

"Oh, I'll let you find out that for yourself," said Joe. "In fact, if I remember your chart right, you have an encounter with her coming up soon."

"Marvelous," I said as I got up to go. "Can't wait."

Time to go home, I thought. So. Saturn was a headmaster, and Neptune ran the fish-and-chips restaurant. That confirmed it. Joe was crazy. Completely crazy. But his craziness suddenly gave me an excellent idea to try out at school . . .

Chapter Seven
Psycho woman

Tuesday lunchtime, and it was time for my appointment to see the school counselor. I was ready. Plan A hadn't worked, but Plan B had begun to form in my brain on the way home last night after seeing Joe.

It's your choice how your life turns out, he'd told me. *Okay*, I told myself. My number-one option was still to get out of here, and, unknowingly, by ordering me to see the school counselor, Mrs. Richards had presented me with a way to do it. I was going to pretend that I was a raving loony. Flies in the attic. Lights on, but nobody home. Crazy. I was going to get myself expelled on the grounds of being nuts. If that didn't bring my dad hurrying back from the graveyard slot, I didn't know what would.

I sat outside the counselor's office going over my act. I would be a little sniffly and occasionally make weird birdlike noises. I would make myself go cross-eyed. I'd let one arm have a life of its own and float up into the air above my head. And I'd drool. If none

of that worked, I'd pretend that I was a teapot.

After around five minutes of sitting there, running through what I hoped would be an Oscar-winning performance, the school secretary came out.

"You can go in now, Danu," she said. "Miss Luna will see you now. Door on the right."

"Umbanga," I said and beamed back at her.

She gave me a strange look, so I winked at her and went through the door that she'd indicated.

"Oh!" I said when I got inside and saw the lady who was waiting for me. "Are you the counselor?"

The lady who was standing by the window nodded her head slightly. She wasn't what I had imagined, although I don't know what I'd expected. Someone who looked professional in dressy clothes like a teacher or a bank manager or something. Not the woman who was in front of me. For a moment, I forgot to do my crazy act because I was too busy gawking at her. She looked like an artist or a gypsy with long, silver-gray, wavy hair, a crescent moon pendant around her neck and star earrings, and she was wearing a silvery silk skirt that matched her hair. She looked like a waif mermaid who had grown legs and had been washed ashore. I waited for her to say something so that I could begin my act, but she didn't. She just stood staring out the window up at the sky. After a while, when she hadn't paid any attention to me, I began to wonder if she even knew that I was there.

I coughed. "Ahem."

She turned to look at me then but still didn't say anything.

"I'm Danu. Your one o'clock. Raving loony reporting for counseling. Yes, ma'am." I saluted like they do in the army and then began to bark like a dog.

No reaction. She just looked at me. Then she put out her arms and began to sway, side to side, front to back. *What the bat poop is she doing?* I wondered. I let her continue for a moment, and then she stopped and sat down. She looked like she was going to cry.

I sat down across from her. She reached out to the table, took a tissue, and blew her nose.

"Well, aren't you going to say anything?" I asked. "Take notes? Give me some advice?"

She sniffed. "No."

We sat there in silence for a while, and then my curiosity got the better of me.

"Um. Aren't you supposed to do something?" I asked. "Say something wise?"

She turned her silvery-blue eyes in my direction. "What? What could *I* possibly say?"

"Dunno. But isn't it your job to *know* what to say or do?"

Her eyes filled with tears. "Say. Do. Is that all there is? Sometimes all I want to do is *be.* It's best just to go with the flow." She rose up from her chair and went to stand at the window, where she tilted her face to look at the sky again. "You know, Danu, sometimes I think, *Is this it?* There has to be more. Otherwise what's it all been for?"

And then to my total and utter amazement, she started to dance. A flowy, hippie type of dance like the kind that we used to do when we were in elementary school and some overly enthusiastic teacher would say, "Everyone be a tree, let your arms be branches, and sway with the breeze."

I watched her with my mouth hanging open for a few moments before it dawned on me. *Ah. Yes. I get it,* I thought. *She's trying to outloon me. Yes, she's smart, this one. She knows the stunt that I was going to try, and she's trying to outdo me. Well, ha! I figured it out, and I'm not giving up here.*

I got up and joined in her wacky dancing. I could dance like a loony, too. "Yes. Yes. Come on, let's be trees," I said, as I waved my arms in the air and bent my knees. "Bending in the wind, this way, that way. La la la la la la laaaaaaaaa."

"Not trees," she said, as she pranced around the room. "Water. Dance like the water, flowing; the tides go in, the tides go out. Go with the flow,

Danu, go with the flow."

She must have done some strange, experimental counseling course where they teach this as a new approach to try with difficult students. *Fine with me*, I told myself as I followed her lead.

"Water. Flow. Right. Can do," I said, and changed my tree dance to the sea dance, which actually looked pretty similar and consisted of me wiggling my hips and waving my arms from side to side in the air.

We danced around the room for a few minutes like a pair of demented hippies, and then she stood up on one of the chairs. "If I stretch high enough, I can reach the stars."

Omigod, I thought when I realized that she was showing no signs of giving up either. *What if she really is bonkers? In fact . . .*

"Excuse me, Miss Luna, but are you really the school counselor?" I asked.

She looked down at me from the chair. "I am, and I'm not. I don't think that we should define ourselves by what we do. Do you? I mean, do you feel that you are just a student."

"Goodness, no. I'm much more than that."

"There you are, then. So don't ask stupid questions."

"Okay," I said, and sat down to try and figure

out my next move.

Miss Luna finally got down off the chair and sat on the couch across from me.

"So," she said.

At last, I thought. *She's done with trying to act crazier than me, and we're going to get down to business.* "So . . ."

And then she burst into tears. First a few sobs, and then her chest began to heave . . . and heave. *Wow*, I thought. *This lady really is a psycho woman. She's not playing a game.*

I handed her the box of tissues. "Is there anything I can do, Miss Luna? Should I call someone?"

"Oh, no, no." She continued sobbing but took a tissue. "Just . . . please . . . please don't tell anyone . . . just I'm not feeling like myself today . . . and please call me Selene, not Miss Luna. That sounds so grown-up."

"Oh, okay. Selene. I won't tell anyone. I promise. Now. Do you want to tell me what's wrong? It can't be all that bad."

Selene, or Miss Luna, laid back on the couch, flicked off her shoes, and began to tell me all about how she felt, how it wasn't easy for her being so affected by the waxing or waning of the Moon.

"Every two days the Moon changes signs," she sobbed. "If it's not waxing, it's waning, then it's full, half moon, then new moon, crescent. Never a day off to relax."

I had no idea what she was talking about, but I listened patiently. The more I listened, the gist of it seemed to be that she was having the same problem that I was. She didn't like everything changing all the time either. I didn't know what to say, but talking did seem to help her, so I let her continue. Every now and then I would interject by saying, "Uh-huh. And how do you feel about that?"

At the end of my hour, my "counselor" had calmed down. She looked at her watch. "Oh, time's up," she said. "Thank you so much. You've been marvelous. I feel . . . well, almost . . . more cheerful about things."

"Anytime," I said as I got up to leave. "Call me anytime you need to talk."

"Thank you sooooo much," said Selene. "I will."

And then it dawned on me. Tides. Waxing. Waning. Moons. Joe had told me that I might have an encounter with the Moon. He couldn't have meant Miss Luna, could he?

"Hey, you don't, by any chance, know Joe Joeve who runs the deli, do you?"

Selene nodded. "*Diu Pater*. God father. Of course. Everyone knows him around here."

"And um . . . you don't, by any chance, think that

you're the Moon, do you?"

She laughed as if I'd said something really stupid, then she nodded again. "Of course I do, because that's who I am. But how did you know?'

"Joe told me that my horoscope said that I had an encounter with the Moon today. I didn't know what he meant, though. He's been telling me a lot of things that I don't understand, actually."

Selene beamed at me. "Of course! You're a Zodiac Girl. You are, aren't you?"

"Zodiac Girl, Queen of Sheba, or a demented chicken. I'm still trying to decide."

Selene looked perplexed. "Pardon?"

"Okay," I said. "Um . . . I'll put it this way, if you think that you're the Moon, then, yes, I'm a Zodiac Girl."

I wonder how many people there are in their club, I asked myself. What Joe had told me about people being planets and the Moon was beginning to make sense. They obviously belonged to a club that was into astrology, and each one of them got a nickname when they joined–like, you be the Moon, you be Mars, I'll be Venus–in the same way that anybody might like to dress up and pretend to be their favorite characters. My friend Jane was obsessed with Harry Potter and belonged to a club back home where all of the members dressed up as characters from the books. Jane got to be Hermione Granger one Saturday a month. So Joe, Miss Luna, Hermie, and the others, they weren't crazy. Maybe a little eccentric. That was all.

"I thought that you were unusually perceptive," said Selene. "Most of the students here can't see what's in front of them. But you can. Yes. I should have known that you were a Zodiac Girl. Now everything makes more sense."

A little, I thought as I got up to leave. Miss Luna is another member of a strange club along with a bunch of others who like to pretend that they are celestial beings. Why not? At least it made life more interesting, and I did feel marginally better after my counseling session. Maybe Miss Luna's "dance-like-the-sea" therapy had something going for it after all.

Chapter Eight

Cakes

What an insane day, I thought as I let myself into the apartment after school. I went into the kitchen to put my supplies on the counter. I'd been thinking hard about everything that Joe had said to me at our last meeting–about how, if you want a home, make it yourself. And the quote about knowing what you could change and what you couldn't had made more sense after talking to him. Once Joe had explained it, it seemed obvious, and I didn't know why I hadn't thought it before. So, okay, maybe I couldn't change the fact that I had to live here a little longer and I couldn't change the fact that I had to go to a new school, but I could change how it was living with Aunt Esme. I could make her cold, unwelcoming apartment more of a home, and as Joe had suggested, I was going to start with some baking. I'd been to Mr. Patel's store and bought all of the ingredients that I thought I'd need for making cakes. Chocolate cakes were my favorite, so I'd bought a large bar of dark chocolate, butter, flour, sugar, milk, powdered sugar, pecans, and cherries.

I glanced over the recipe that Joe had given me, and, as instructed, I switched the oven on to 375°F.

I laid out all of my ingredients on the counter in the order that I'd need them and then looked for a cookie sheet. Nothing. I went from cupboard to cupboard, but there was little there: just a couple of plates, two bowls, three mugs, two wine glasses, two water glasses, and one box of my breakfast cereal. I felt so disappointed because I'd been looking forward to my first attempt at being a super chef. I was about to turn off the oven when I spotted a drawer under the oven door. I pulled it open, and, luckily, there were a couple of cookie sheets and a cake pan in there. All pristine, never been used. *They must have come with the apartment*, I thought. Aunt Esme would never go out and buy something that you needed to cook with in a million years.

Another quick check of my supplies, and I was off.

When Rosa arrived with my dinner at 6:00 P.M., she sniffed the air in appreciation.

"Making the cook?" she asked.

I nodded. "Cooking. Making cakes. I am. Almost ready. Want to try?"

She shook her head as if she didn't understand, so I acted out eating and pointed at the kitchen. She nodded her head.

My cake was almost ready, and I'd followed the directions perfectly, and, judging by the lovely, buttery chocolate smell, they were going to turn out fine. I could hardly believe how good the simple exercise of baking had made me feel. It reminded me of home when I used to help Mrs. Wilkins. And the time had flown by. Usually the hours when I got home from school were the worst, when I felt the most lonely, but this time, I'd been so busy that I'd hardly noticed being on my own.

Rosa came and stood by the kitchen door, so I pointed at the oven, crossed my fingers, and made an anxious face. She laughed and sniffed the air again.

"Smell goods."

When the timer on the oven buzzed, I opened the door and took out my cake. It had risen beautifully and looked perfect. Rosa did a little clap, so I gave her a bow.

It was nice having someone in the kitchen. My second visitor in a week. I looked at Rosa and pointed at the kettle. "A cup of tea?"

She nodded and smiled. "Thanks to you."

I made us some tea, and, when the cake had cooled, I put it on a plate and took it into the living room. Rosa followed me but seemed hesitant to sit down.

"No, please," I said, indicating that she should.

She sat on the edge of the sofa, took a piece of

cake, and bit into it.

"Very, very goods," she said, and smiled at me.

I took a piece too and tried it. It *was* good. The dark chocolate had melted beautifully to make bursts of liquid chocolate in the middle. Delicious.

As we sat there munching, I realized that Rosa and I had never exchanged more than two or three words in all of the time that she'd been coming to the apartment. I'd been so angry with Dad and Aunt Esme that I'd taken it out on her, too. But it wasn't her fault that I'd been left alone, and as we sat there, I began to wonder what her life was like. She didn't speak very much English, so she must have felt alienated at times, like me.

"Where do you live, Rosa?" I asked. I pointed at her and then acted out going to sleep.

"Ah," she replied. "Sleeping. I sleep . . ." She said and pointed out the window in the direction of the apartments above Mr. Patel's store at the other side of the square.

"And your home?"

She looked at me quizzically.

"Home," I repeated. "Family. Is your family there?"

She didn't understand, so I went to get my wallet and took out the photo that was taken of Dad and me in the yard last summer. "Family. Me. Dad," I said.

Her face suddenly looked sad, and she shook her head. "No. No family here. Family Poland."

I nodded. "You have friends here?"

"Cousin Halina. She nice lady. She work here, too. No see much." She then pointed at me. "You? Family is where?"

"Mom died when I was three," I said, but Rosa looked puzzled. "Dead. Kaput." I acted out someone having their throat cut, which she clearly didn't understand. So I acted out someone being shot in the head, which caused her to look even more confused. I lay down on the floor with my eyes closed and then acted out someone stabbing me with a knife. Rosa looked horrified.

"Murdering?" she asked.

I shook my head vigorously. Mom had been sick, but she died peacefully in her sleep. *Maybe I should have thought of a more subtle way of acting out being dead*, I thought. Then I had an idea. I raced to my room and got a few sheets of paper. I drew a male stick figure getting on a plane.

I pointed to the drawing and then the photo of Dad.

"Dad," I said, and Rosa nodded.

Then I drew a female stick figure under the ground with a cross above her. Rosa nodded. I think she understood the fact that Mom wasn't here anymore. And finally, I drew a smaller stick figure for my brother and showed him to be near the building by the sea reading a book. "Brother, college," I said.

"Understand. College," Rosa said, and smiled and then took the pen and paper. She drew a mother, father, and three little girls. "Sisters," she said. Then she drew $$$ signs and pointed to herself. "I work, send money."

I nodded. So she was away from her family, too. I wondered what her life was like back in Poland and whether she missed her friends and family and if she had any pets. I drew a dog, a cat, and a horse. She nodded and drew two cats. She looked sad when she drew them.

We looked at each other, and I put my hand on my heart. She put her hand on hers. *We understand each other completely*, I thought, *even though we don't have all the words. She's lonely too.* I resolved to make time for her in the future when she brought my dinner. I'd been so selfish grumbling like a miserable brat when all this time she had been missing her home and family just like me.

After she'd left, I cleaned up the kitchen, left a piece of cake out for Aunt Esme, and then went to my computer to check for e-mails. Only one from my brother, who had finally remembered that I existed.

Hey, Danu. Sorry I haven't been in touch. Let me know if you need anything. Take care of yourself.

Luke.

Pff, I thought. Hopeless. He's as bad as Dad. Head in the clouds and nose in a book. He's studying ancient history and isn't very interested in anything or anybody else.

I quickly wrote a group e-mail to Annie, Fran, Bernie, and Jane, letting them all know what I'd been up to, and as I was finishing up, my zodiac cell phone rang.

"Hey, Danu," said Joe. "Go to the site. There's a competition on there that's just your thing. First correct answer wins. And according to your chart, Pluto is coming square into your fourth house."

"Doh. Which means what?"

"Oh, right. Pluto is the planet of transformation, and your fourth house is the house of home. So it sounds fated that you will win, doesn't it? Don't waste any time. Bye."

I went to the astrology site, and, just as Joe had said, a pop-up window appeared, inviting me to take part in a competition.

Answer this question and win a makeover for your home from the top stylist P.J. Vlasaova and his team of wonder workers.

Excellent, I thought, *Joe is really on the ball.* First his excellent idea about baking and now this. If I win a home makeover, I could make a difference to this place and cheer it up a bit. And what's more, it could be a surprise for Aunt Esme.

I looked to see what the question was.

"*Dui Pater* is another name for what?"

Easy peasy, I thought as I typed in my answer: Jupiter.

Chapter Nine
Bad boys

School was uneventful for the rest of the week because I behaved myself for a change and kept quiet in class. I still hadn't made any real friends there, but people certainly knew who I was now: the girl with the big mouth. The girl who gives the teachers a hard time. The girl who put trick soap in the teachers' bathroom, turned the swimming pool bright red, etc., etc. But nobody knows who I really am behind the tough-girl act. I'm still the lonely girl. I wished that Sushila was in my class because, even though she has tons of friends, she always stops to talk if she sees me in the playground or at the bus stop after school.

"Hey, Danu," said Marie Marshall who sits behind me in math class. "Got any more good tricks up your sleeve?"

I shook my head. "Nah. That phase in my life is over."

"So, what next?" she asked.

"Not sure," I replied. "I might run for Congress,

but I might also join the army. Whatever. You'll have to find someone else to entertain you when classes are boring."

Marie's face looked hurt for a second. "I was only asking," she said. "No need to be sarcastic."

The bell rang, and she flounced out to recess with her friend. *Stupid, stupid,* I thought. Why had I snapped at her like that? She was only being friendly, but I hadn't given her a chance. We could have had a nice, normal chat about what I was going to do next. I was *so* looking forward to it. My "get-myself-expelled" plan hadn't worked. My "act-like-a-crazy-person" hadn't worked. So I was ready to embark on Plan C. I was going to stop resisting and fighting against what had happened, I'd decided. I was going to go with the flow, as Miss Luna would say (but without the hippie dancing). I'd try to accept the situation and make it better little by little. Joe had said that it was up to me to make the changes, and that's what I was going to do. Make some changes–starting with the apartment.

So far, it was all coming together beautifully. A couple of days after I'd entered the competition on the website, an e-mail had come through saying that I'd won, and the day after that, I got an e-mail from the design team asking when I'd like them to come over.

"Next Monday," I wrote back. "And it has to be done in a week."

Aunt Esme was flying to New York on Sunday night. Rosa was coming to stay. We had the week of my school break to finish the apartment before she got back.

The timing couldn't have worked out better. I couldn't wait.

After school, I stopped by the Patels' store to get supplies for a carrot cake that I wanted to try out. I wanted to get home before the rainstorm began that had been looming all afternoon. Already the wind was stirring, making the square seem even colder and more unfriendly than usual. As I was walking toward our apartment building with my purchases, I decided to call Joe to check out something about the recipe. I pulled out my phone and dialed his number. Big mistake. A bunch of boys were hanging around the ball sculpture in the middle on the square. One of them spotted my phone and nudged one of the others, who looked my way. I could tell immediately that they were going to cause trouble.

"Hello, hello?" asked Joe on the other end of the phone. "Is that you, Danu? Is everything all right?"

"Yes. No. Um. Got to go."

I quickly put away the phone. I should have

known better. Our teachers were always warning us about keeping hidden any items that anyone might want to steal when we were out in public, but it was too late—they had seen it.

One of the boys nodded at one of the others, and he glanced my way and then nodded back. A feeling of sickness hit the pit of my stomach. They were going to try and get me. I could feel it. I quickly counted them. One, two, three, four, five. *Should I run back to the store?* I wondered. Or *try and make it up to the apartment? Better decide.* The boys were coming toward me. *Oh God, oh God. So much for being a Zodiac Girl and it bringing me luck*, I thought. *My zodiac phone is just about to get me into trouble.*

I glanced over at the boys. They were getting closer. *Run or fight?* I asked myself, as fear flooded through me. *Run, run*, said a voice in my head. But my feet weren't moving. Suddenly from somewhere deep inside, my fear turned into anger. I'd had enough of feeling that life was against me. Abandoned by Dad. Ignored by Aunt Esme. Left out by the girls at school. Enough! I'd had enough, and I wasn't going to take any more—especially from a bunch of pimply boys who were after the one nice present that anyone had given me in ages. *Fight*, said a voice at the back of my head.

I shoved the phone deep in my pocket, leaned on

one hip, and turned to the boys.

"Want something?"

"Yeah," sneered a tall boy with long, greasy hair. "Gimme yo' phone."

I gave him my best Nurse Torturer withering look. "*Give me* your phone, not 'gimme,'" I said. "'Your' not 'yo'. That's the correct way to say it, you stupid boy. Now repeat after me. Give me *your* phone."

One of the boys snickered, which seemed to annoy the tall boy.

"Shaddup, Benny," he growled.

"*Shut* up," I said, and looked around as if in exasperation. "Didn't anyone teach you boys to speak properly?"

For a moment, the boys were stunned into silence. It looked as if nobody had ever spoken to them like I had, and part of me couldn't believe my nerve. But it didn't take the tall boy long to regain his cockiness. He gave me a look like I was a piece of dirt and then walked toward me and shoved my shoulder. "I said, gimme yo' phone."

I knew that I was asking for trouble because the other thing that our teachers said is that if one of us is ever mugged or picked on, just hand over whatever it is that your assailant wants because your life is worth more than a watch or a phone or whatever's being stolen. I knew that it was true, but

I wasn't in a sensible mood. I felt angry, and I wasn't going to take being pushed around. I tried shoving the boy back, but two of his friends grabbed my wrists and held them back. By now, my heart was beating really fast and my earlier courage was beginning to fade. *Why, oh, why doesn't anyone like a police officer walk past when you need them?* I thought.

The ringleader reached for my pocket to try and grab my phone. I wiggled away so that he couldn't reach. He tried again. Since my arms were pinned back, all I had to fight back with were my legs, so I gave him a quick kick in the shin.

"Oww!" he cried and bent down to rub his leg, and then he laughed an evil laugh, stood upright, and looked at me as if he was deciding what to do with me next.

"Seems like we've got a fighter here, Trev," said the chubby one named Benny to the tall boy as I kicked out again and struggled to get free. "A fighter with no brain."

Trev laughed again.

"It's you who has no brain," I said. "You're pathetic picking on a girl who's all alone."

Trev looked around as if he was pleased with himself. "Um . . . I don't think so, little girl. Five of us. One of you. You do the math."

"I have," I said. "And it adds up to COWARDLY."

The tall boy scowled and attempted to reach for my pocket again as I wiggled and squirmed and tried to get away from him. But it was no use–there were five of them. They were all closing in on me, and I was getting weaker. I closed my eyes and felt the boy reach into my pocket and begin to pull out the phone. I was about to tell them to take the stupid phone and just leave me alone, when suddenly I felt one of the boys being pulled off me.

"I DON'T think that's yours, son," said a familiar voice.

I opened my eyes. It was Joe. And, boy, did he look angry.

"Joe!" I cried. I'd never been happier to see anyone in my whole life.

Joe bowed. "At your service, Danu," he said.

Trev laughed. "*At your service*," he mimicked. "Yeah, right, old man. Get him, guys."

The boys released me and lined up, ready to attack Joe. My heart was pounding away in my chest by now, and I could hardly breathe.

I leaped onto Benny's back. "You leave him alone," I said.

Benny shrugged me off like he was discarding an unwanted jacket.

Trev laughed again. "Or else, what?"

Oh God, I thought. *Or else, what, indeed?* There were

five of them and only two of us, and Joe was by no means young or healthy-looking with his round belly.

But something was starting to happen to Joe.

He took in a deep breath and seemed to grow in size. Like someone was pumping him up like a bicycle tire. He grew and grew. His belly began to shrink, and his stomach appeared flatter. His shoulders grew broader. He seemed to be growing younger by the second. And taller. And no, yes . . . he was sprouting a beard! I rubbed my eyes. *This can't be happening*, I thought as I watched Joe transform in front of my eyes into a lean, mean, fighting machine. *A lean, mean, fighting machine with . . . no, no way, I can't be seeing this!* I told myself. Joe's top half looked like a young athlete, but his bottom half . . . his bottom half . . . *It can't be* . . . looked like a horse! *No. Not possible.* I rubbed my eyes again and felt like I was about to faint. I leaned back against the nearest wall to recover and catch my breath. At that moment, there was a loud boom of thunder, a crack of lightning, and the skies began to pour down rain. In the dim light, it was hard to see exactly what was going on; it was all happening so fast. *I must be imagining it*, I thought as I watched Joe, or someone very similar to Joe, flex his muscles and charge into the lineup of boys like a quarterback. I stood aside and watched as one boy went flying toward the bus

stop with the flick of a hand. With the kick of a hoof, another boy was tossed into the middle of the square as if he weighed nothing; a third boy stared at the half-man, half-horse that was Joe with horror and then took off as fast as his legs could carry him, leaving only Trev and Benny behind.

"Way to go, Joe," I said in admiration from the wall as they cowered in front of him.

"You want to stay, boys?" asked Joe, looking down at them as a magnificent fork of lightning lit up the sky, followed by the deep boom of thunder.

Benny took off after his friends, leaving only Trev. He and Joe stood facing each other, sizing each other up like cowboys about to have a showdown.

Suddenly, Trev yelled, "Freak," and made a run for Joe. Joe chuckled, put his hand out, and held him back by his forehead. Trev frantically punched the air in front of him, but as hard as he tried, he couldn't get any closer. As his strength diminished, he began to look scared. He took one last look at Joe, turned on his heels, and fled.

"You okay, Danu?" asked Joe as Trev disappeared around a corner and out of sight.

"Uh, yeah . . ." I nodded, and this time, I couldn't stop it. I fell to the ground in a faint.

When I woke up a few moments later, I saw that Mrs. Patel was running toward us through the rain.

"I saw what was happening from the store. I have called the police," she said. "They are on their way. Danu, are you all right?"

I looked around for Joe. He had returned to his usual form and was standing to my right, looking at me with concern.

"You fainted," he said.

"Ma . . . wuh . . . buh . . . huh . . ." was all that I could stutter. "H . . . Horse . . ."

"Horse?" asked Mrs. Patel as she knelt down and put the palm of her hand on my forehead.

I pointed up at Joe. "Horse. Jupiter. Archer . . ."

Joe shrugged like he didn't know what I was talking about.

"I think that she may be delirious," said Mrs. Patel. "Maybe she was hit by lightning. We should get her home."

Joe nodded.

But I was sure that I wasn't delirious. Nor had I been hit by lightning. Nor had I imagined what I had seen. I'm not prone to hallucinations. Not normally. Joe had transformed himself right in front of me, and it had sure as heck blown a hole in my theory that he was an innocent eccentric who belonged to a club of similar loonies who liked to dress up and pretend that they were celestial beings. Oh, no. What I had witnessed a few moments ago

was waaaaay out of the ordinary. He had looked like a god. He had fought with the strength of ten men. And a horse. *It couldn't be true, could it?* I asked myself as I sat up. *It couldn't. Had Joe told the truth, and he really was Jupiter? No. Not possible. It's crazy. Or is it?*

As the police sirens got closer, I closed my eyes, sank back to the wet ground, and allowed myself to be carried home.

Chapter Ten

Makeover madness

"When are they getting here?" asked Sushila as she appeared at the door first thing on Monday morning.

"Any minute," I replied. "Rosa and I are just having breakfast. Want some coffee or juice or something?"

Sushila nodded and stepped inside. I'd told her on the bus coming home from school all about the makeover people, and she had asked if she could be here when they came because she loved watching makeover shows on TV.

I felt so excited. Better than I had in ages. The apartment makeover was the first thing that I'd ever won in my whole life besides a hamper of German sausages when I was ten and was going through my vegetarian phase. My prize this time was going to be a lot more useful.

I led Sushila through to the kitchen where Rosa was making coffee and reading the Post-it notes that I'd left all over the kitchen for her. I introduced the two of them and then found a mug for Sushila.

"Kenyan or Colombian coffee?" I asked.

"Just coffee," said Sushila.

"And a cookie? We have pecan or chocolate. And we also have cake. Homemade by me," I said proudly.

Our kitchen was now stocked like a normal kitchen, because before she left, I had asked Aunt Esme if I could do some grocery shopping online for food and stuff. She had been in such a hurry getting ready for her trip that she agreed, and I'd had a great time with her credit card. Think big, Joe kept telling me, so I had. I'd stocked up the kitchen with all sorts of goodies. Rosa had helped me and ordered the basics like bread, cheese, pasta, vegetables, fruits, and so on. We had found a great site that had pictures of the food as well as the prices, so she would point to items and I'd click on them to go in our basket.

"What's going on?" asked Sushila when she saw the Post-it notes.

"I'm teaching Rosa English," I said. Last night we had decided that it would be a good idea after our slow attempts at communication with the stick-figure drawings. Instead of drawing pictures, we were using words on Post-it notes and then sticking them onto the correct objects. Like DOOR on the door. JELLY on the jelly. Rosa was a quick learner and already could say most of the things in the kitchen.

As we made the coffee, the doorbell rang.

"Design man coming," said Rosa to Sushila, who nodded back at her as we trooped out into the hall.

I opened the door to three peculiar-looking people. A serious-looking blonde girl in heavy black glasses and hair pulled back in a bun, a stocky man with a shaved head who looked like a construction worker and was carrying a big case, and a tall, thin man with long, wavy, dark hair, a hooked nose, and skin so pale that he looked sick. They were all dressed from head to toe in black.

"You are Danu?" asked the thin man.

I nodded.

"I P.J. Zis is my team, Natalka and Oleksander. You may call zem Nat and Alex."

I must have looked confused because the team standing before me looked more like they worked in a funeral home than an interior design agency.

"*Ve're* your prize! Ta-daaaah!" said P.J. without a smile, and then he clapped his hands and ushered Nat and Alex inside. "Vy you iz staring at me?"

"Oh, sorry," I said as I stepped aside so that they could come in. I hadn't realized that I had been staring, but there was something about P.J. Despite his nose and pale skin, he was incredibly handsome, like a romantic poet from another era. And he spoke with a foreign accent that I was trying to place. It sounded half Russian, half something else.

He tossed a long velvet scarf over his shoulder and swanned in, walking up and down the corridor, looking at the walls, the ceilings, the floors.

"So. Let's see vot ve 'ave here," he tutted as if he didn't like what he saw.

The name P.J. rang a bell. "Hey. Do you know Joe Joeve?" I asked.

P.J. turned and nodded. "Everee-*one* knows Joe. Ve call him ze god fazer. My studio iz on ze same street as 'iz café. Best kebabees in the area."

"And are you one of his planet club?"

"Planet club? Vot is this?"

"You know, Jupiter, Venus . . ." I didn't want to say too much in front of the others in case they thought that I was crazy, plus, I didn't know how much Alex and Nat knew about the possibility of their boss being a planet in his spare time. Since the episode with Joe in the square, I was more open to it being a reality. I'd decided, *why not?* No one really knew who anyone was or where we came from or where we go or what we're even doing here on this planet, so why shouldn't some people in human form be manifestations of the planets?

"Oh, *oui*. Yeah, sure. *C'est vrai. C'est moi*." He clapped his hands. "Some call me P.J., some call me Pluto. Pluto iz ze name, transformation iz ze game.

So vere should ve start? Let's do ze tour!"

"Are you Russian?" I asked.

He flicked back his hair. "Russian, Ukrainian, Plutonese. Votever. I prefer to think of myself as Universal."

Yep, he's definitely one of them, I thought. *He talks in the same riddles. I wonder what he can do and if he's going to turn himself into anything peculiar like Joe did.*

But, no. He was acting reasonably normal. He went from room to room up and down the corridor a few times, *hmm*ing and tutting as Rosa, Sushila, his team, and I followed.

"*Zut alors*," he said when he finally stopped.

"I know," I said as I caught up with him. "It's awful, isn't it?"

"Hmmm. Not awful. Just empty. Each room it says, nozing."

"*Nozing*?" I asked.

"Nothing," said Sushila.

"Correct," said P.J. "Nozing. I ave no idea who lives 'ere. Vot kind of person. Vot zey like. Vot zey don't like."

"That's what I said," said Sushila. "It's unlived in. Like a hotel."

"Exactly. A blonk canvas . . ."

"*Blonk*?" asked Sushila.

P.J. nodded. "Yes. Blonk, blonk . . ."

"Oh, blank?" I asked.

P.J. nodded. "Yes. A blonk canvas. Vich is marvelous. Vere shall ve begin? Alex. Nat. Take notes. Mizz Harvey Jones. Vot vould you like? You von ze prize, so ve do vot *you* vant. Any ideas?"

"Um . . ." I was suddenly seized by a momentary panic. What if we did a makeover and Aunt Esme didn't like it? I had no idea what her taste was really like. As long as everywhere was clean, that seemed to be the most important thing. "Um . . . Aunt Esme likes it neat and clean, so maybe we should go for something simple, uncluttered."

"Ve could," said P.J. "But vot vould *you* like?"

He sat on the sofa and indicated that I should sit next to him. I perched next to him while his team stood behind him, like slaves guarding a pharaoh.

P.J. snapped his long, bony fingers. "Colors, samples," he said, and Nat produced a stack of books from out of a huge bag and placed them on the table. "Okay, Danu and friends. Ve 'ave to make some choices."

We spent the next half-hour looking through fabric samples, paint samples, catalogs of furniture, lights, floors.

"Do you vant traditional, modern, exotic, romantic? Vot do you vant?"

I looked up from one of the books. "Um . . .

something to make it look more cozy. More like a place where people live, not just pass through. Somewhere you'd like to come back to."

P.J. stared off into the distance as if he was visualizing it in his mind. "Yes. I zink ve can do that. Yes. Leave it all viz me, Danu, ve're going to totally transform ze place!"

Oh dear, I thought. *I hope that Aunt Esme will be happy with the results.* It was one thing acting like a sulky teenager. It was another thing redecorating her apartment. Doubts were beginning to set in.

"Um, maybe we should do just one room to start with . . . or maybe even one corner of a room? What do you think?"

P.J. looked at me as if I had slapped him. "I zink zat zere are ozzers who vould have died to have zis prize. I zink zat zere are ozzers who appreciate who I am. And vot I can do." He clapped his hands and Nat and Alex stood to attention by his side. "Come on. Ve're leaving."

As I watched them go, I looked around at the cold, empty room. If I let P.J. go, I'd still be coming back to this night after night. Nothing would have changed. I remembered Joe's words, "Think big." Dare I risk the wrath of Aunt Esme by going for the transformation, or should I opt for not rocking the boat and leaving everything as it was? I ran after them.

"P.J., *P.J.* No. Please don't go. I'm sorry, and I really do appreciate such a great prize. Please stay. Do what you have to."

P.J. turned back from the front door and snorted. "*Pfff!* It's alvays ze same. People resist change more zan anything else." He put the back of his hand on his forehead and looked up at the ceiling with a pained expression. "If only zey knew." He looked back at me. "You 'ave to break down to break through, you know. Can't make an omelet vizout breaking eggs."

"I know. Yes. Yes. Whatever, just don't go. I'm thinking big. I really am. I'm not resisting. Please make an omelet. Let's do this thing!"

P.J. clapped again, and this time, he almost smiled. "Excellent. Ve're going to have some great fun here."

Later that night after P.J. had left, I checked the astrology site to see if there were any other competitions or surprises to look out for.

There was just one word.

Mars.

Now what's that supposed to mean? I asked myself as I got into bed. Mars is the name of a candy bar. One of my favorites, actually, but what could that have to do with anything? Joe was intent on getting me to fatten up a bit. Maybe he was saying to eat more chocolate? No problemo there. Or maybe he meant the planet Mars. It's one of them. I knew them all by heart now. Mercury. Venus. Earth. Mars. Jupiter. Saturn. Uranus. Neptune. Pluto. And, of course, the Moon and the Sun. And I'd been looking them all up in my astrology book. Jupiter was the planet of joy and expansion. Pluto the planet of death, rebirth, and transformation. Venus of love, harmony, and beauty. Now what was Mars again? I knew I'd read it somewhere . . . Mars . . . But before I had the answer, I had drifted off to zzzzzz . . .

Chapter Eleven

Red planet

P.J. was true to his word. At 6:00 the next morning, he arrived with his team. Plus decorators. And carpenters.

By 6:30 A.M., the flat was a hive of activity, with hammers banging and drills drilling. No way could I stay there with all the din, so when Rosa left to go to one of her cleaning jobs, I left, too, with the intention of going to Osbury to see Joe and do some shopping.

"I hope that what P.J. is doing is going to be all right," I said as we stood at the bus stop.

Rosa sighed, shrugged, and, in the same way that I had when I was trying to tell her that my mom was dead, she acted out a gun being put to her head and then someone trying to cut her throat.

"Exactly," I said. "Aunt Esme's going to kill me."

Rosa shrugged again and then smiled. The bus came around the corner, and we both got on. I glanced back up at the apartment building, and I swear I could see things being thrown out the windows and floating down to the ground below.

I closed my eyes quickly and prayed that they weren't throwing out any of Aunt Esme's favorite things.

When I got to Osbury, I went straight to Joe's deli to get some breakfast and to see if he had anything in store for me.

"Zodiac Girl reporting for duty," I said with a salute when I spied his smiling face behind the counter.

His face lit up when he saw me. "Danu. Sit. Eat."

A few minutes later, he had put down a plate piled high with scrambled eggs, bacon, hash browns, and toast in front of me. I told him about P.J. arriving and how he seemed to have taken over the apartment, and he nodded as if that was exactly what he expected.

"That's what Pluto does when it touches a chart," he said. "It is the planet of transformation. Of death and rebirth."

A fleeting feeling of panic went through me, and I prayed that the death wasn't mine when Aunt Esme returned from her trip.

When I had finished breakfast, I planned to go and look around the stores. It was my school vacation, after all, and I needed a break from my bad-girl act at school. It had been very tiring. However, Joe had other plans. As I ate the last mouthful, he handed me a piece of paper and then checked his watch.

"You're just in time–the class starts in ten minutes,"

he said and pointed out the window. "Out to the street, turn right, and it's in the community center."

"Class? But, Joe, it's my vacation," I moaned, but then I glanced down and read the leaflet.

Are you puny?

Picked on?

Kicked around?

Hair pulled?

Bullied?

Had enough? I bet you have.

No need to suffer.

You can put an end to it all with Mario's Martial Arts.

I teach kung fu. Tae kwon do. Hara-kiri. Karate.

No experience necessary. All ages and sizes welcome.

Osbury Community Center, Tuesday. 9:30 A.M.

Be there. Or be pathetic.

"*Hara-kiri?*" I asked. "Isn't that a way of killing yourself with your own sword, Japanese style?"

"It is," said Joe with a chuckle. "Mario can be a tough taskmaster when someone irritates him. In the past, he used to overreact to students who didn't pay attention, but don't worry, he's mellowed out slightly. I doubt he'll be forcing anyone to do hara-kiri here. What he will do, though, is teach you to defend yourself."

"But I have you, Joe," I said. "You can do that 'turn yourself into a centaur' thing if I'm in trouble."

Joe raised his finger to his lips. "Shush. We don't want that getting out. I'm not really supposed to do that in public, but those boys . . . well, they annoyed me . . ."

"Remind me never to annoy you . . . or this guy Mario," I said. "Although it was pretty cool when those boys saw you . . ."

"It was, wasn't it?" said Joe as he beamed. "Got rid of them, all right. But I am only your guardian for a month. You have to learn to defend yourself."

I nodded. *Interesting*, I thought. He hadn't denied what I had seen the other night. So it wasn't my imagination after all.

"Why me, Joe?"

"Why what, Danu?"

"Why am I a Zodiac Girl?"

Joe looked at me with a gentle expression. "Same reason that you have the hair you do, the eyes you do, the personality you do, and the experiences you do. It's in your chart. Usually being a Zodiac Girl happens at a turning point in someone's life. A make-or-break time. The planets conjoin to assist you, but after that it's what you make of it."

"I see," I said. I was certainly at a turning point in my life. No doubt about that.

Joe cleared away my dishes. "Go on, then. Off you go."

I wasn't going to argue. Before he had come to my rescue the other night, I had felt scared, despite my tough act. And the moment that the boys had pinned my arms back had replayed over and over in my mind when I'd tried to go to sleep later that night. What I should have done. What I should have said. How I should have reacted. I knew that I wasn't as in shape as I used to be when I lived at home with Dad and played lots of sports at school. Plus, I'd lost a lot of weight since moving in with Aunt Esme and her lettuce leaves. The one thing that I did know, though, was that the experience the other night in the square with the boys wasn't one that I wanted to repeat. The next time I wanted to be strong and fight back with confidence.

I got up and took up a kung fu stance. "Ah, so, here I go," I said with an Eastern accent and karate-chopped the air.

"Just asking to be hara-kiri-ed," Joe said with a laugh. "Now get over there."

I made my way to the community center, and when I got inside, I saw that the class had already started. A group of around ten people were sitting on mats while, in front of them, one of the most striking men I had ever seen paced up and down. He was tall with skin the color of dark chocolate and dressed in black sweatpants and a sleeveless T-shirt that revealed well-toned muscles in his arms.

I jumped as he yelled, "AGAIN!", at someone on the mats.

"Yes, sir!" a skinny young boy in the front row squeaked.

"YES, SIR!" said the man as he put his face close to the young boy's. "Let's have some ENERGY, YOU MOUSE OF A MAN!"

The boy pulled back and looked like he was going to cry. "Yes, sir," he squeaked again.

I closed the door quietly behind me and began to tiptoe in so that I would not disturb the class. As I was attempting to creep toward the seated group, the man at the front stopped. Without even turning in my direction, he boomed, "WHAT time do you call this? You're LATE."

"Oh. Yes. Sorry. Um . . . I only just found out about the . . ."

He turned around. He really was remarkably good-looking, like a Hollywood movie star. Deep brown eyes, wonderful cheekbones, and a chiseled jaw. He was almost too good-looking to be real, and I felt myself blush as his gaze brushed over me.

"Rule number ONE. I like my students to be on TIME. Understood?"

"Yes, SIR," chorused the gathered audience.

"You. Dreadlocks. Sit!" He shouted at me like a drill sergeant.

Pff, I thought, *no need to be nasty. Just shows that looks aren't everything.*

"RUUUULE two. I like my students to look NEAT. We'll be working in close proximity. Noooooooooo dreadlocks whipping around. You. What's your name?"

"Dee, sir,"

"Deeser? What kind of name is that?"

"No, sir. Dee, sir. Short for Danu."

"So why did you say Deeser? Don't you know your own name?"

"I was being polite. Calling you sir, sir."

He hesitated for a moment before roaring, "Cor-RECT. Now sit and get rid of those dreadlocks before the next class."

You might be impressive to look at, I thought, *but I'm not going to take that from someone I've only just met who's not even a teacher at my school.*

"Why should I, sir? They're clean."

"They don't suit you," he said. "You're a very pretty girl, and you're doing yourself no favors."

"I . . . ah . . ." I was speechless. That wasn't the answer that I'd expected. And part of me felt flattered that he'd said I was pretty.

"SIT!" the man suddenly boomed at me.

“Sit, sit,” whispered a weedy-looking boy to my right as he pulled on my hand. “If you get him mad, he takes it out on us in the exercises. Pleeeeeease.”

The boy looked like he needed all the help he could get and I didn’t want to make life difficult for him.

“Sorry, sir,” I said, saluted Mario, and sat down.

“Sooo. As I was saying before we were so rudely interrupted. My name is Mario Ares. This is my class. I work you hard, but I get results. No pain, no gain. By the time you all leave here, you will be experts in judo, Thai boxing, jujitsu, aikido, kendo . . .”

“Hara-kiri,” I called out before I could stop myself. Being troublesome in class had clearly become a habit.

Mario fixed me with a cold stare. “Okay. You. Stand. Approach.”

“Now you’re in trouble,” said the skinny boy next to me.

I strode up to the front.

“Okay, Dreadlocks,” he said when I reached the front. “Introduce yourself to the class.”

I turned to face the assembled group, which consisted of two very fat boys, three very skinny boys, two boys with bright red hair and very pale skin, two old ladies–one dressed in a pink sweatsuit who was obviously infatuated with Mario, the other

who looked like she had broken her leg–and an Indian girl who looked around Rosa's age.

"I . . . my name is Dee, short for Danu. Harvey Jones."

I went to sit down.

"And why are you here?" asked Mario.

"What–like on the planet or here in this community center?"

"Don't you talk back to me, young lady. I meant here in the community center."

"To learn self-defense."

"SIR," bellowed Mario.

"SIR," I bellowed back.

"Now hit the deck," said Mario.

"*Hit the deck?*"

Mario pointed at the floor. "Give me twenty, you girlie wimp."

"*Girlie wimp*?" I felt outraged. I wasn't girlie. And I wasn't a wimp. No one was going to speak to me like that.

"Do them yourself," I replied. "And if anyone's the girlie wimp around here, it's you."

The group gasped in horror.

"Exactly what I thought when you walked in here," said Mario. "Brat. Spoiled brat. Bet you always get your own way, don't you?"

"What are you going to do if I don't do them?

Give me detention? Expel me?"

Mario narrowed his eyes and fixed me with a cold stare again. I stared back. I was good at staring contests. I could make my eyes go out of focus and do it for ages. I had been the best at my last school. Plus, I felt angry with Mario. Just who did he think he was? I had come to a self-defense class. Not to join the army. I turned around to leave.

Mario dismissed me with a flick of his hand and turned his back on me. "Go on, then. Run away, little dreadlocked princess. Have your own way. No time for time wasters here."

It was then that I read the logo on the back of his shirt: *Red Planet Martial Arts.*

I should have known, I thought. Red Planet. Mario was Mars.

Chapter Twelve
Worms

I felt close to tears when I got out of the class. I ran to a bench on the other side of the park, away from the sidewalks that were now full of morning shoppers. *What a horrible man*, I thought. He didn't know me at all, otherwise he wouldn't have said those things. *Girlie wimp? Wimp?* I wasn't. No way. I had been really brave when Dad had left. I hadn't cried at all after he'd hugged me good-bye and then picked up his suitcase and gone out to the taxi that took him to the airport and the *other side of the world*. It was only later, when I was in my room with Snowy and Blackie, that I had let the tears flow. And even though I wanted to, I hadn't cried when I'd said good-bye to Mrs. Wilkins when my taxi had arrived to take me to Aunt Esme's a couple of days later. I knew that it would upset her too much if she saw me crying. And I hadn't cried when I said good-bye to Fran and Annie and Bernie and Jane. I knew that they'd be upset, too. They were all crying like real girlie wimps when the car drove me away. But not me.

No, the only time I lost it was when I had to say good-bye to Blackie, Snowy, and Spot. How was I going to explain my disappearance to them? I could tell that they knew that something was going on because Blackie kept getting into my suitcase every time I tried to pack and Snowy would sit on the end of my bed, looking at me with big, sad eyes. On the morning that I left, I'd given Spot an apple and then gone and sat in the middle of the yard behind our old house with Blackie and Snowy on my lap for a last hug and then I'd howled like a baby. Although, so did Blackie and Snowy. We were a trio of howling howlers. But I'd been brave other than that. I'd been brave the first time I found myself alone at Aunt Esme's with no company except for the TV and the dead plant on the balcony. I'd been brave when I started school and everyone was running around saying hi to their friends and not one person asked who I was or what I was doing there or tried to make me feel welcome at all. And I'd been brave when Trev and his horrible friends had tried to steal my phone. So, girlie wimp? How DARE he! He had no idea what I had been through. And to call me a spoiled brat and a princess on top of all that. I hated him. And I hated Joe for having sent me to him. He was supposed to

be my guardian and be looking out for me, not introducing me to cruel, insensitive meanies.

I got my astrology book out of my backpack and looked up Mars.

Associated with physical energy, stamina, or goals, it said. *Often depicted as a warrior.* Well, Mario fit the bill perfectly.

From my bench, I watched people strolling up and down the street, stopping to gaze in windows, going in and out of the stores. Going into Europa for a sandwich. Going about their lives. Girls from my school. Some with their friends. Some with their moms. Suddenly I felt like I was going to cry. I didn't even have a mom to go shopping with, never mind a dad who didn't seem to care what I did.

Above me, the sky was getting darker, threatening rain, and I realized that I was cold. I only had a fleece jacket since the weather had been warm when I'd left the apartment this morning. I got up to go home and then realized that I couldn't. P.J. was there doing the makeover.

Nowhere to go. No one to talk to. The song that Joe had sung when I first met him ran through my head. "Nobody likes me, everybody hates me, think I'll go and eat worms. Big ones, small ones, fat ones, thin ones, see how the little one squirms."

At that moment, I spotted a worm wiggling its

way along the ground. It looked so pathetic. And so small. I felt like picking it up and taking it home to take care of. *Don't worry*, I said out loud. *I won't eat you.* Then I thought, *God, I am sad. Now I'm talking to worms!*

I sat on the bench a while longer and tried to decide what to do. I could call my friends back home on my normal cell phone. But they'd probably all be out having a life. Hanging out and enjoying the school vacation. Speaking to them would only make me more homesick. So would talking to Mrs. Wilkins. I didn't want to go back to the deli in case Joe asked how the self-defense class had gone, and I couldn't take any more criticism. I scanned the stores in front of me. The magic store? I could pop in and see Uri. No. He's too wacky. Not in the mood for him. Mars, Joe had said. He must have seen an encounter with Mario in my chart. Definitely not in the mood for him either, so no way am I going back to his class.

At that moment, my zodiac phone beeped to say that there was a text message for me. I looked at the screen. "Transformation is a process. Before the butterfly, first the caterpillar and the cocoon."

Another one of Joe's riddles, I thought as I got up and stomped some warmth into my cold feet. *Pff. Well, I hate riddles and I hate astrology, and I'm not going to let it or them control my life.*

Suddenly I had a brain wave. Okay, so maybe some of the planets were around in human form. Well, I was going to pick and choose who I wanted to see, not the other way around. Pentangle. The hair and beauty salon. That was it. It was run by the beautiful blonde lady who had been in the deli on the day that I met Joe. Unlike Mario, she looked gentle. Joe had said that she was Venus, and at the time, I'd thought that he was a raving lunatic. Well, I knew better now. I found the page on Venus in my book. Planet of love, harmony, and beauty, it said. *And about as opposite to Mars as you could get*, I thought. Just what I needed. Joe might say Mars. Well, *I* say Venus. I would go in there and treat myself to a manicure or a facial or something. A little bit of pampering in a friendly environment. Heaven. Fran, Annie, Bernie, Jane, and I used to play beauty salon on Sundays when it was raining and there was nothing else to do, and I'd always enjoyed it. I had some spare money that Aunt Esme had left me, and it would be an enjoyable way to stay out of the apartment until the decorators left.

Feeling much happier now that I had decided to take back control of my life, I got up and made my way over to the salon.

A young girl with spiky red hair was behind the counter when I opened the door and stepped inside.

"Um . . . is the lady with blonde hair in today?" I asked.

"Nessa? Nah. She's at the suppliers with Trace," said the girl as she looked me over. "What do you want done? Your hair? It's a bit of a mess, isn't it?"

"No. I wanted a mani–" I caught sight of myself in the mirror. My hair *was* a bit of a mess. More than a bit. The front was all frizzy from the rain, and my dreadlocks looked . . . dreadful, like straw-colored sticks stuck to the side of my head. I looked like a crazy girl. No wonder no one wanted to be my friend. "Yes. My hair."

"Okay," said the girl. "I guess I can do it for you."

I glanced back at my reflection in the mirror and took a deep breath. "Yes. Okay. Thanks."

She led me to a chair, sat me down, and tutted as she examined my hair. "Oh dear, oh dear, oh dear . . ."

"Can you just comb it out?"

The girl looked doubtful. "It could take hours."

"I have the time if you do."

"Sorry, darling, but your hair's ruined. It's too far gone."

I looked at my reflection in the mirror. After months of being happy to look how I felt–the odd one out–suddenly I couldn't bear it one second longer. I wanted to look like me again. Dee. Normal.

The girl must have seen my look of disappointment.

"Look, dear, tell you what. I have an idea, but you're going to have to trust me. I've just taken a class and learned this fabulous new technique. You'd be perfect for trying it out on."

I glanced up at her. She looked sincere. I nodded, closed my eyes, and a few minutes later, all I could hear was the *snip-snip-snip* of scissors cutting hair.

"Done," said the girl a little while later.

I opened my eyes and shrieked. "OMIGOD! *Omigod!* Bat poop and a half! What have you done?"

If my appearance was strange before, it was even stranger now. I looked like I'd just joined the army and been given a crew cut. There was hardly any hair left on my head. "What's this supposed to be? The porcupine look? I look like a bristle-head. I thought you said that you'd learned a fabulous new technique?"

The girl looked offended. "I have. And it looks better than it did and . . ."

I got up from the chair and ran toward the door.

"Hey. I haven't finished," the girl called as I ran out. "And you haven't paid . . ."

I didn't care. I looked awful. I ran for the bus and kept my head down until it pulled up. Once I was on, I made a dash for the back and prayed that I didn't see anyone that I knew. I felt in shock. At least with the dreadlocks, I looked like I had some style, some edge. Now I looked like I had just had the worst haircut ever. Which I had. My plan was to get back to the apartment and hide in my bedroom for the next few years until my hair grew back.

Life cannot possibly get any worse, I thought miserably as I let myself in through the front door half an hour later.

The apartment looked like a bomb had hit it.

"Oh nooooooooo," I wailed. "What happened?"

Floorboards were up, revealing the joists underneath. Walls were stripped of wallpaper, exposing the plaster and electric wires underneath. Cupboards in the kitchen had been pulled off the wall, leaving ugly gaps in the paint, and it even looked like someone had attempted to knock down the wall between the kitchen and the living room.

"Oh my goodness. I'm a dead girl," I moaned as I surveyed the disaster that was left of Aunt Esme's apartment.

P.J. appeared out of the bathroom. "Oh, you're back," he said cheerfully as he checked out my hair. "Hmmm. Interesting haircut."

"I wish I could say the same for your decorating," I said as I slumped to what was left of the floor and surveyed the wreck. All the fight had gone out of me. I didn't care about anything anymore. My life was over.

Chapter Thirteen
Visitors

"Break down to break through," said P.J., who didn't seem at all phased by my reaction. "Transformation iz a process . . ."

"Before the butterfly, first the caterpillar and the cocoon," I finished for him. "Can't you guys come up with any original sayings of your own?"

P.J. looked hurt. "But iz true and that iz my saying. Everyone's alvays using my sayings," he said with a pout. "Iz because I say such vise things about life and death all ze time . . ."

"Never mind that. The place is a mess. What am I going to tell Aunt Esme when she gets back?" I demanded, as visions of Aunt Esme in full freak-out mode played through my head.

"You von't need vords," said P.J., who was clearly still feeling sulky. "Ze apartment vill speak for itself."

"Oh, yeah? And what's it going to say? Um . . . had a little party while you were away. Sorry about the holes in the wall . . . and the ceilings . . . and the floors."

P.J. flounced off. "You 'ave no faith. Just you vait and see. And if you're crossing ze room, be careful to walk on ze joists and *not* to stand on ze areas between ze joists, as ze plaster isn't solid and you'll go straight down to ze floor below."

"I'm not stupid, P.J.," I said as I tiptoed along one of the joists like a professional tightrope walker to see what they had done with my room. At least the floor in the hall and my bedroom was still intact, although half of the ceiling had been taken down, and someone had painted big daubs of different colors on the walls. When I caught sight of myself in the little mirror above the dresser, I quickly turned it back to the wall, then got onto my bed and snuggled under the covers, where I intended to stay until my hair grew back.

I must have nodded off, because the next thing I heard was the sound of Rosa's voice.

"Dee, Dee, you is in there? Is time for eatings."

"Go away. I'm not hungry."

"Aunt says Dee must eat. Aunt called."

I stuck my head out. "Aunt Esme called?"

Rosa's expression when she saw me reminded me of how bad my hair looked. I darted under the covers again. "What did you say to her?" I asked from underneath the covers. "You didn't tell her about the apartment makeover, did you?"

"Best no, I am thinking. Is great messingness out there. What is happening with the hair?"

"Oh, disaster, Rosa," I said, as I poked out my head. "You might as well see it fully. Bad, bad haircut."

Rosa calmly surveyed what was left of my hair, and then her face broke into a smile. "Is better, I am thinking. Can seeing the face more. You be pretty girl."

I sighed. "Except for the fact that I look like a boy."

"Growing back, it will," said Rosa. "Coming to eat. Kitchen is no more for cooking. I got pizza."

At the mention of food, my mouth began to water. "What about the apartment destroyers? Have they left?"

Rosa nodded as I got out of bed. "Back morning time," she said, then she giggled. "More destroying then."

"I don't think there's much left to demolish," I said, as I followed her into what was left of the apartment to eat our dinner in the middle of the chaos.

Later that night, I settled down in my bed, and Rosa went off to Aunt Esme's room, where she was staying while Esme was away.

Because I had slept so soundly earlier, I felt wide awake. As I tossed and turned, I became aware of the night sounds. The whistle of the wind in the windows. A train rattling past in the distance. A dog barking. Somewhere down below, someone shouting. A car alarm going off. And then silence. Not even the sound of a clock ticking. Only my breathing. In. Out. In. Out. Then the sound of . . . what was it? Footsteps. On the stairs. Someone trying to be very quiet but not succeeding. *Probably the people upstairs had a late night*, I thought. But no. The steps had stopped. On our floor. I waited to hear a key in the lock and the sound of the door to the apartment across from us open and shut as the lady who lived there went inside. But she was away, too, wasn't she? I seemed to remember Aunt Esme saying something to Rosa about it. And come to think of it, the footsteps hadn't sounded like hers, either. She always wore high heels, and they made a clickety-click noise on the concrete stairs. These footsteps were more solid, and they had sounded like a couple of people. Males. I strained to hear anything else. My heart began to pound as I heard a scraping sound in the hall outside. *At our door*, I thought as I sat bolt upright. *Omigod! Someone's trying to get in!*

I held my breath so that I could hear every tiny sound. Yes. There it was again! A scraping, fumbling sound. It would start and then stop.

I decided to get up to go and see if Rosa had heard

anything and was awake too. I got out of bed and tiptoed across the room. I opened the door as quietly as I could and crept into the hall. There was definitely someone outside. The scraping sound was louder in the hall, like someone was trying to pick the lock.

My heart was pounding like a drum as I crossed the hall. Who could it be? Maybe Aunt Esme was back early from her trip. No. She had a key. Maybe whoever it was thought that the apartment was empty. With all of the activity during the day, that was highly likely. The people who lived around here were always telling stories of construction workers having their tools and equipment stolen on unmanned sites. Empty apartments broken into when occupiers were away. I heard the murmur of conversation outside, so I strained to listen. Whoever it was was whispering, but I knew the voices. It didn't take me long to place them. It was that bully, Trev, and his stupid friend, Benny. Anger flooded through me. How *dare* they try to break into where I lived! I crept into Aunt Esme's room where I could see the dark shape of Rosa asleep in the bed.

"Rosa, Rosa," I whispered, but she was sound asleep. Outside in the hall, the rustling noise continued. If one of them was picking the lock, then they might succeed any minute, and what would they find? A young woman who barely speaks English and a puny-looking girl with a bad haircut. *Oh, I wished that I'd stayed in Mario's class and learned some self-defense techniques*, I thought as my heart continued to pound in my chest and my mind began to fill with terrible images of what might happen. *Maybe this is why Joe sent me to the class. Maybe he's not so bad after all. He must have known that we were going to be burglarized, and he and was trying to ensure that I could protect myself. Oh, rats. Why didn't I do what I was told?* I could just see the newspaper headlines: Teen with strange name and haircut murdered in her own bed by local thugs. She fought back, but like a girlie wimp.

Oh, God, what should I do? I asked myself. "Rosa," I whispered again and shook her ankles to wake her up.

She woke up with a startle. "Wha–?"

"Shhh," I hushed her. "Someone's trying to get in the front door."

Rosa hid under the covers. "Tell them go away. Go away now."

"But, Rosa, you're the grown-up. You tell them."

"I scary. No like dark either. Tell them go away."

I could see that Rosa wasn't going to be any use. It was up to me. I went into the hall. What should I do? I didn't want to say anything, in case they realized that it was me and that I couldn't fight back.

Get something to hit them with, a voice in my head said. I tiptoed along to the living room to try and find a hammer or a pickax. Unfortunately, I forgot that the floor was up and there were only wooden joists across the room. I stepped onto an area between the beams, and CRASH, my left leg went straight through the thin plaster of the ceiling below.

"Owwow!" I yelped before I could stop myself.

Behind me, Rosa had crept into the room. She was carrying a flashlight and shone it in my face. "What you is doing?" she asked.

"Taking a bath. What does it look like I'm doing? I'm stuck. Oh, God. Rosa, hold onto me."

Between the two of us, I managed to free my leg and climb onto one on the joists, then get back into the hall where the floor was still intact. I glanced back into the living room; light was streaming up from the floor below. I knelt down and looked through the gap to see the corridor downstairs.

Rosa began to giggle. "Good job not falling into downstair people's beddings. They be getting heart attack if someone falling in from ceiling."

Her shoulders began to shake with laughter.

"Shhhhh. Rosa. This isn't the time for jokes. In case you'd forgotten, some idiot is trying to break in."

"Yes. Me having idea. Turning on light and noise. They thinking many people here."

It wasn't a bad idea, and I hadn't thought of anything better, and I could still hear the sound of someone at the door. Luckily, there were three locks since Aunt Esme was very security-conscious and had made the apartment as safe as she could.

"Okay, let's go for it," I said, and turned on the hall light. Rosa ran back into Aunt Esme's room and reappeared with a radio, which she turned on loud. Luckily, it was a talk show, not music.

I crept back into the hall and put my ear against the door. The fiddling, scraping noise had stopped. I listened. Rosa turned the music up and then called out loudly, "Jacob, hurry up in the bathing room!"

And then she replied to herself in a deep voice. "Be outing in a minute."

I gave her a thumbs-up and listened at the door again. Finally, finally, I heard steps retreating.

"They gone?" asked Rosa.

I nodded, and she came over to me and gave me a big hug. It was only then that I started shaking, and Rosa had to put a blanket around me and make a mug of hot chocolate before it would stop.

We both slept in Aunt Esme's big bed that night, but neither of us got much sleep.

Chapter Fourteen

Yes, Sir!

"Oh, you again," said Mario with a smug look when I got to his class the next day. I was the first person there, and this time I was determined to stay, no matter what insults he threw my way.

"Yes, SIR," I said.

He glared at me to see if I was joking around, but I stared him back eyeball to eyeball and didn't flinch once. I was dead serious, and I think he got the message.

"Okay. You can start by taking your cap off," he said.

"I . . ." I was about to object because I had worn a black baseball cap to hide my hair disaster. I took it off. I didn't want him throwing me out for disobeying him.

He didn't even try to disguise his reaction. "Good God Almighty!" he said as he gasped with horror. "What happened to your hair? Thinking about joining the army, are you?"

"No, SIR," I said. "Bad haircut, SIR."

"You can say that again," he said.

"Bad haircut, SIR!"

He gave me another penetrating look to see if I was joking but, once again, I met his gaze. "Nessa will fix it," he said. "Report to Pentangle one night after class."

"Yes, SIR!" I said, although I had no intention of going back in there. What could they possibly do to make it better besides shaving my head and giving me a wig? No. I would wear a baseball cap until it grew back.

The rest of the class began to filter in and take their places on the mats that Mario had set out on the floor. I glanced at them as they took their places. It was exactly the same group as yesterday.

"Okay, then, you ugly bunch of losers," Mario started when everyone was seated. "This is the class that gives you the skills to survive. It will make you into prettier specimens. Now, I want to have an atmosphere of trust here, so I'd like you all to get up and introduce yourselves to this creature here who has crawled in off the sidewalk." He checked my face to see my reaction to his insults, but I just smiled back at him. *Call me what you want*, I thought. *This girl ain't budging*. "I know you did it yesterday," he continued, "but you're going to do it again. Why? Because I say so. Each one of you, up, say your piece, and then back to your place because I don't want to spend all day on this." He motioned to a chubby blond boy to get up.

"Name?" asked Mario when the boy got to the front.

"Matthew."

"And you're here because?"

"Kids laugh at me at school. Call me fatso. Tubs. Had enough, sir."

After Matthew was another fat boy. "Name, Cuthbert. Same as Matthew, had eeeeeeenough, SIR."

The old lady in the pink sweatsuit got up next. "Nancy. Used to be a victim until I came to these classes. Poor me, little old lady. Not anymore. Thanks to Mario, I'm rough and I'm tough, and no one's gonna get me on a dark night and steal my purse. No, SIR!" And she did a couple of high karate-type kicks and ripped her pants. "Oops! No problem. I've got another pair in my duffel bag." As she dashed off to change, I swear that I saw Mario's face almost twitch with laughter, but he soon recovered his stern expression.

The other old lady with the broken arm and bandaged leg got up. "My name's Lily, and someone *did* get me on a dark night. There were four of them. Troublesome boys who smelled like beer. Never again. Let me tell you all about it and my operations, ooooh I can tell you some stories–ooooh, my leg, my

arm, the pain, the pain, my arthritis, awful, it is . . ."

"Good for you, Lily," interrupted Mario. "You can fill everyone in more on your operations during the break. Today I'll be showing you how you can use that cane of yours as a weapon."

"Bring it on," said Lily, as she held her cane in the air and shook it at an imaginary assailant.

The three skinny boys were next. Archie, Paul, and Ian had similar stories. iPods stolen, cell phones taken, teased at school, picked on for being puny.

"Don't worry, boys, a few more sessions here, and the bullies will run a mile when they see you coming," said Mario as the boys beamed back at him. "Archie, I rename you Axman; Ian, I rename you Iceman. Paul, I rename you . . . Paul the powerful. Now, toughen up, you big girls!"

Last up was the pretty Indian girl. "Usha's my name. Same story. Picked on for being a different color. People call me Curry Head or tell me to get back to Thailand, which is very insulting because my family is from Kerala in southern India. I want to be able to walk down the street without feeling scared."

"You got it, girl," said Mario, and then he nodded his chin at me. "Okay. So, good. Okay, now you, no-hair girl."

I got up and went to the front. "Last night someone tried to break into the apartment where I live. I was really, really frightened, and although we scared them off, if it ever happens again, I want to be able to defend myself. Also, not long ago, some kids tried to steal my cell phone and would have succeeded if a friend hadn't showed up. I'm here to learn to fight back."

"Excellent," said Mario and then clapped his hands. "Now, on your feet you horrible group! Let's get strong!"

Everyone got to their feet, even Lily, who wobbled up with the help of Matthew and Cuthbert.

"Are you puny?" yelled Mario.

The assembled group moved around on their feet and looked at the floor as if it held the answer.

"For heaven's sake, get some ENERGY, you lazy people. 'NO, SIR' IS THE ANSWER. Now let me hear you."

"No, SIR," we attempted.

"AGAIN!" roared Mario. "Are you losers?"

"No, SIR."

"A bunch of big girls?"

"NO, SIR," we roared back at him.

"Are you fighters?"

"NO, SIR!" yelled Ian who wasn't thinking about what he was saying, "I mean, YES, SIR."

"YES, SIR," the rest of us joined in.

After exercising our lungs, Mario made us run

around the room, march in place, touch our toes, and stretch our muscles.

"Okay, everybody," said Mario after we'd warmed up enough, "up on your feet and let's see how you walk. Just relax and walk like you normally do."

We did as we were told, and after a few laps of the room, Mario clapped his hands. "Enough!" he called. "Back to the mats."

Once again, we did as we were told.

"Paaaaathetic," said Mario as we sat in front of him. "Bunch of victims, all of you, Nancy excluded. But no wonder the rest of you have been picked on. Matthew, you waddle. Cuthbert, you walk like a frail old man with bad knees. Ian, you've obviously spent too much time in front of your computer with those slumped shoulders. Stop slouching. Paul, you walk like you've got ants in your pants. Dee–head held up high. Walk boldly. Archie, you look like you're begging someone to come and beat you up. Oh, poor me, poor little me. Anytime soon someone's going to get me. WELL, NOT ANYMORE. Get up again. Get some attitude in your head that says, I am confident. I am in control. DO NOT MESS WITH ME."

We stood up, and glancing around, I could see what he meant. We did look like a puny group waiting to be pounced on.

"What do I hear? I said, WHAT DO I HEAR?"

Mario growled.

"YES, SIR!" we shouted back at him.

"Okay," said Mario. "Now I want you all to imagine that attached to the top of your head is a helium balloon and attached to the bottom of your spine is a lead weight."

I did as he directed and felt myself grow two inches. It felt amazing. I glanced at the rest of the group, and already I could see that we were all standing taller.

"Okay, with that image in mind, go. GO. Walk. One, two, three. Noooooo. Ian, relax. All of you, *relax*. Shoulders down. No slouching. Up straight. In charge." Leading the way, Mario began to walk around the room like he was leading us into battle. I really got into it. It felt good to be walking as if I owned the world, not as if I had the weight of it on my shoulders.

The rest of the morning flew by. We did more warm-up exercises and then started learning some defense techniques. Mario showed us how to block anyone coming in for an attack by using our arms or our legs and, in Lily's case, her cane. We learned vulnerable points on the body and how to target them. How to use our elbows, feet, knees, and hands by making a claw, using the heel or side of our hand, clenching it into a fist, and using the knuckles. I never realized that I could do so many things with just my hands. It was totally amazing. The heel of a hand to someone's nose can do some serious damage. And a foot to the groin even more, especially if the assailant is male! Matthew got a bit carried away with that move and kneed Cuthbert with too much force. Poor Cuthbert had to hobble off to the side to recover, and for a while, I didn't think that he was going to rejoin the group. In the end, he did and seemed relatively unharmed except for the fact that his voice had gone up a few octaves.

During the lunch break, I checked my zodiac phone. There was a text message.

"Jupiter meets Venus," it said.

I decided to call Joe to ask him what it meant.

"Hey, Danu," he said when I got through. "How you doing? Meet Mario?"

"I did. I have, I mean, someone tried to break into the apartment last night."

His voice sounded concerned. "You okay?"

"I am now, but I was scared at the time . . ."

"It isn't in your chart that you get hurt," said Joe. "I would have warned you."

"I thought that's maybe why you had sent that message saying 'Mars' and sent me to Mario's classes."

"Not exactly. All I could see was that there was an

encounter with Mars in your chart. How that manifests itself is up to you."

"I don't understand. You mean that it's not all predetermined?"

"Some of it is, some of it isn't."

"Jooooooe, don't start talking in riddles again. What do you mean?"

"How you respond to events in your life, that's not determined. That's completely up to you."

"Ah . . . You mean like seeing a glass as half full or half empty depending on how you view it and what mood you're in?" I asked. Mrs. Wilkins always used to say that back home.

"Sort of. It's back to sink or swim, the choice is yours. You can sulk and moan and be miserable about your situation, or you can get up and do something about it. Which I know you are beginning to do. How's the apartment coming along?"

"Looks like an earthquake hit the building. Maybe I'll say what you've just said to me when Aunt Esme gets back and sees that her apartment's ruined and starts frothing at the mouth. Oh, Auntie, I will say, it's your choice, swim or sink, you can either see this as a disaster and moan about it or you can be glad and respond with joy. At which point, she will clobber me over the head and probably kill me. So, yeah, thanks for those words of wisdom, Joe."

Joe began laughing on the other end of the line. "I'm sure your aunt will be fine about it. In the meantime, enjoy the class with Mario."

"Enjoy! Ha. You wouldn't say that if you had seen what he's making us do this morning."

Joe laughed. "Ah, but he's a great teacher."

At that moment Mario came to the door and called everyone back in. I noticed that he clocked my phone and raised an eyebrow.

"Quick, Joe, your message," I said as I got up off the wall that I'd been sitting on. "What did it mean, Jupiter meets Venus."

Joe just laughed. "You've got the book. You figure it out."

"Jooooooooooe . . ." I objected.

"Danu," called Mario. "In here, NOW."

It was no use. I could tell I wasn't going to get Joe talking, and Mario looked like he was in a mean mood. I closed my phone and went back in.

"Okay, you sniveling bunch of wimps," said Mario as we all took our places, ready for the afternoon session. "Who's going to be my next volunteer to be mashed up by the master?"

I raised my hand. "Me, SIR!"

I hadn't had as much fun in ages.

* * *

On the zodiac site that evening, there was a message from Mario:

There are only two types of people in this world. The quick and the dead. Winners and losers. Successes and failures.

That's six, I thought. *These planet people really can't count!* But I knew what he meant, and I knew which one I wanted to be. The one who was alive–without too many bruises!

Chapter Fifteen
Conga

My school break seemed to go by in the blink of an eye. Rosa and I fell into a routine of up early and out of the apartment, Rosa to her job and me to the class with Mario. In the evening, to keep out of the decorators' way, Rosa would come and meet me at Joe's, where we'd have dinner and then we'd see a movie and then home to bed. Sometimes Sushila would join us, too. And on a couple of evenings, her friends Amy, Chloe, and Joele from school turned up with her. It seemed that I wasn't the only one who wanted to get to know new people. In fact, Joele and Amy said that they had wanted to get to know me better from day one, but they had been intimidated because I always seemed so aloof, like I didn't need anything or anybody.

In the self-defense class, my skills improved daily, and by the Friday afternoon, I could even throw Mario to the ground. At first, I thought that he was letting me, but he swore that he wasn't.

"I'm a good teacher," he said, as he got up from the

mat where I had knocked him down with a leg lock.

Regardless of whether he was letting me win or not, I felt a million trillion times more confident and walked out of his last class on Friday afternoon feeling like I could take on anyone.

Best of all, though, was that I discovered what "Jupiter meets Venus" meant. Or at least meant for me.

I was about to go into Joe's after my last class when guess who was coming out of the deli? Nessa. She took one look at me. "Zodiac Girl?" she asked.

I nodded, and, without another word, she had me by the collar and was dragging me into her salon.

"Oh, nooo," I pleaded. "Please. Not after last time."

"Trust me," she said, and almost threw me into a chair by the sink. I could have arm-locked her and tossed her to the ground, but I decided not to resist. *Why not trust her*, I thought, *I don't have anything to lose. At least not any hair, anyway.*

I closed my eyes and let her do her work. She put on some spacey music, and after all the physical exertion of the week, with the soothing touch of her hands as she washed my hair and the lavender scent of the shampoo, I soon drifted off. When I woke up and looked in the mirror later, I could hardly believe my eyes. A girl with shoulder-length, glossy blonde hair stared back at me.

"Wha–?" I stuttered. "Is it a wig?"

Nessa tugged on the hair, and I winced. No. It was definitely connected to my scalp. *Maybe she's a witch as well as a planet in human form*, I thought.

"Magic?" I asked.

"Sort of," Nessa said, and grinned back. "Hairdresser's magic."

"But . . . how . . .?" I started.

Nessa showed me swatches of different colored hair that she had on a sample card by the mirror. "We can do anything these days. Good, isn't it?"

"Really good," I said and nodded. I swished my new hair around like I was in a shampoo commercial. It was a huge improvement on my "sergeant in the army" crew cut, and it felt great to look like the old Dee again.

Jupiter meets Venus. Jupiter is the planet of joy and expansion. Whatever it touches grows. Venus is the planet of love, harmony, and beauty. The two meet, and what do you get? Bingo. Hair extensions.

I laughed all the way to the bus stop.

Back at the apartment an hour later, I opened the door, expecting to see the usual dust and debris. Before I could even step in, P.J. had pounced on me.

"Close your eyes, close your eyes," he said, as he

covered my face with the palm of his hand.

I quickly did as I was told, and he led me down the hallway.

"Okay, looking now," he said. "Ta-daaaah."

"Surprise!" yelled a chorus of voices.

"*Omigod*," I said with a gasp as I opened my eyes to see Mr. and Mrs. Patel, Joe and Rosa, Uri, Mario, Nessa (*How did she get here so fast?* I wondered), Nat and Alex, Sushila, Joele, Chloe, and Amy all standing there in front of me with big grins on their faces.

"Wha–?" I blustered.

Rosa came over to me and put her arm around me. "Look. Looking around you," she said.

If I had been shocked by the transformation of my hair, it was nothing compared to the change in the living room. It looked fabulous. The walls had been painted a soft honey color, and there were light gold muslin curtains on the windows. The old faded carpet was gone, and in its place was a polished light oak floor. The bookshelves had been filled with books, which at first glance, were a mixture of fiction and travel. My favorites. In the fireplace, the empty vase at last had flowers in it–large stems of yellow roses. A two-seater honey-colored sofa had been added adjacent to Aunt Esme's cream Italian sofa, which had finally had its wrapping taken off it and been strewn with the softest-looking pillows in the same color as the smaller sofa. The whole effect was warm and stylish.

"There's more," said P.J., as he took my hand and led me into the kitchen. That, too, had been transformed. He had left the units where they were but put new light oak doors with silver handles on, which gave the room a modern look. The walls had been painted bright yellow with shiny green and gold tiles on the splashboard areas, which made the room look bright and cheerful. Best of all, though, was when Rosa came in and opened the cupboards and drawers to show that they had all been stocked with utensils, silverware, pots, pans, plates, cups, saucers, basic food, and, in one gleaming storage container on one of the surfaces were cookies, cakes, and chocolates.

As Rosa gave our guests drinks and snacks from our newly decorated kitchen, P.J. showed me around the rest of the apartment

In the bathroom, he had gone for minimalist and modern. It was all white tiles, white walls, and one entire wall of mirrors, which made the room look twice the size that it was.

"As it iz such a small space, I took out zat old bath and put in a shower," said P.J. "You are liking?"

"Fabulous," I said as I looked around. No detail had been left out. A silver towel rail, a shelving unit holding big, white, fluffy towels, a shelf full of amazing-looking scented bath lotions, potions, and soaps to try out, and a touch of color with a bunch of purple freesias in a small vase on the ledge above the sink. "Absolutely amazing."

I grinned at P.J. as he led me to look at the bedrooms. Rosa had been sleeping on the floor in my room for the last few nights while they worked on Aunt Esme's room. I felt full of anxiety as I opened the door because this was the room that was the most important that they got right. I shouldn't have worried. P.J. had worked his magic in there, too, and picked a soft lavender color for the walls and sky blue for the blinds. The effect was simple, cool, and clean–a reflection of how Aunt Esme liked to dress. I was sure that she was going to love it.

"And last, your room," said P.J.

As we crossed the corridor to my room, I thought that he couldn't have done much since he'd only had one day in there because Rosa and I had been sleeping in it. Once again, I was wrong about P.J. In my tiny room, he'd managed to create more space by putting in a loft bed that you climb up to with a ladder. It meant there was an entire area of space underneath. In the space was a desk with my computer, a chair, and bookshelf. On the wall across from the bed were posters of all the places that I wanted to visit someday: India, Africa, Europe,

South America. The Moon. Jupiter. And on the bookshelf next to the desk, there were photos in brightly colored frames. There was one of Spot, Snowy, and Blackie. One of Fran, Annie, Bernie, and Jane. One of my dad and one of Mrs. Wilkins.

"Rosa showed me your photos," said P.J. "I hope you von't mind, but I vanted to put zem vere you can see zem every day to remind you zat you're not alone."

"No, I don't mind at all. P.J., thank you so much . . ." I felt at a loss for anything else to say and was relieved when Uri appeared in the doorway with a shopping bag.

P.J. gave me a low bow. "You iz most velcome. Iz your birthday. Iz good present, no?"

I felt a lump in my throat. "I thought that everyone had forgotten," I said.

"Forgotten? You iz Zodiac Girl. How we forget? No. No vay. Now. Iz party time," he said, and produced a box full of silly party hats, poppers, and blowers. When we joined the others back in the living room, we soon had the hats on. When Nessa suggested that we do a conga line around the apartment, it seemed like the perfect thing to do. We lined up, with Joe in the lead wearing a Napoleon-type hat and a patch over his eye. We put our hands on the person in front's waist, and off we went.

"Ta dah dah dah dah dah da-aaa, ta dah dah dah

dah daaaaaaaaaaa," we sang at the top of our lungs and kicked our legs out to the right and then to the left as we danced down the hall, back around the living room, then back into the hall–just in time to see Aunt Esme come through the front door with her suitcase.

She didn't look amused.

Chapter Sixteen
Freaky deaky

I tried to explain. I really did.

"Mr. and Mrs. Patel and Rosa you already know," I said after she'd thrown everyone out and had fully taken in the makeover. "Sushila, Amy, Joele, and Chloe are from school, and I would have thought that you'd be *glad* that I'm making friends."

"And the others?" asked Aunt Esme.

"The others? Yes . . . well, that's what so totally amazing, and I know it might sound a little strange, I found it kind of weird in the beginning, but they are . . . um . . . um . . . celestial beings . . ."

"*Celestial beings?*"

I nodded. "Yes. Celestial beings who have manifested in human form and live around here."

Aunt Esme didn't look impressed.

"And what's even more amazing, they're all my personal friends."

She gave me a look of great disappointment and began to walk toward her bedroom.

"Honestly," I said as I trooped after her. "Nessa is

Venus, and she runs the beauty salon. Uri is Uranus. He runs the magic store and the Internet café. Mario is Mars and teaches self-defense. He's really cool when you get to know him. And Joe, he's my favorite. He's my personal guardian for a month because I'm a Zodiac Girl. He's Jupiter, and he runs the deli."

Aunt Esme had looked at me in despair. "Zodiac Girl? Mars? Venus? What are you talking about? That chubby man is Jupiter!? You'll be telling me that Neptune owns the bakery next."

I burst out laughing. "No. He runs the fish-and-chips restaurant. It's called Poseidon. You know, Poseidon, Neptune, god of the sea. I looked it all up in my astrology book."

Aunt Esme gave me another exhausted look. "In that case, the Moon would run the cheese store, then?"

"As if! No. She'd be hopeless at that. The Moon is Miss Luna. She works as a counselor at our school, and between you and me, she *is* a bit loony. Of course, there are a few others that I haven't met. I saw Hermie once in the deli–he's . . . what is it? Oh yeah–the manifestation of Mercury and works as a motorcycle messenger, and he's very, very handsome. Saturn is a school principal somewhere . . ."

While I'd been talking, Aunt Esme's expression went through a kaleidoscope of emotions: disappointment,

disbelief, outrage, and concern. In the end, she put up her hands. "Enough! Enough, Danu. Of *all* the things you've done to try to upset me, this has to be the most insane."

"But, Aunt Esme, this is true. It really *really* is."

"Enough, Danu. I don't want to hear another word. Now go to your room."

"But . . . but . . . you haven't even said what you think of the makeover yet. Your room. The living room. Isn't it all fabulous? Don't you love it?"

Aunt Esme looked around her, and her mouth did that shrinking thing it does when she's angry. "Love it? *Love* it? Danu, I don't know how this all happened, but how am I supposed to pay for it?"

"But, Aunt Esme, it's free. See, I haven't told you about P.J. yet. He's Pluto, which is the planet of transformation. I won him in a competition . . . well, not him, but a makeover for the apartment to be done by him. He works as an interior designer. So nothing to worry about. Don't you love it?"

Aunt Esme pointed at the door. "Danu. Go to your room while I think about this and what to do next. *Now!*"

I did as I was told and spent the time in my new work area e-mailing my old friends. I had been terrible about keeping in touch with them while P.J. and his team had been in the apartment, and there were tons of e-mails from all of them, asking where I'd disappeared to and not to forget them. As I started replying to them, part of me felt annoyed with Aunt Esme. Not a word of gratitude, and she hadn't even bothered to come and look at my room.

After ten minutes, I heard a knock.

"Danu, I'm going out for five minutes to get some cigarettes."

"But you don't smoke."

"I do now. I've just decided."

I heard the front door open and close and went back to my e-mails.

As I was writing, a pop-up window flashed up on the left-hand corner of my screen. It was from Joe. "Quick, follow your aunt," it said. "She needs you."

Ha! Just shows how little he knows Aunt Esme, I thought. *She doesn't need anybody*. Then I remembered what Joele had said about me and how I looked like *I* didn't need anyone or anything. Could Aunt Esme possibly be the same, hiding behind her tough exterior?

I got up and walked through the apartment to the window in the kitchen that looked out over the square. It was wet, dark, and windy, but there didn't seem to be anyone else around. I saw Aunt Esme come out of Mr. Patel's store and begin to cross the square. She seemed okay. Maybe Joe meant that she needed me to be more patient with her or something.

I was about to turn around and return to my room when a movement on the other side of the square caught my eye. I strained to see. Someone was over by the alley that led away from the square. My heart skipped a beat when I realized who it was. *Oh, nooooooooo.* It was the terrible twosome, Trev and Benny, and they were creeping up on Aunt Esme.

I raced to my room and called Joe on my zodiac phone.

"Danu. You got my message?" he asked.

"Yes, and you were right," I said as I headed out of the apartment and ran down the stairs two at a time. "Aunt Esme's in trouble. Those boys who tried to steal my phone are after her."

"How many?" asked Joe.

"Two, I think, but the others may be there, too, so hurry," I urged him as I reached the ground floor at full speed. "Can you come and do that centaur thing?"

"You can take them," said Joe and hung up.

"Jooooooooooe . . ."

Too late. He was gone, and the boys were almost up to Aunt Esme, who was walking ahead of them, totally oblivious. I shoved my phone into my pocket and burst through the double doors out of our building, just in time to witness them grab her from behind.

She shrieked and dropped her bag.

"Leeeeeeeeeave her ALONE!" I yelled.

When Aunt Esme saw me, she looked even more horrified. "Danu, turn around. Get back inside."

Trev turned and saw me heading toward them. He immediately began to sneer. "Well, if it ain't little Miss Dreadlocks with the fancy phone," he said, and quickly looked around the square. "Lost your locks, have you?"

"None of your business," I replied as I came to a halt.

"So, where's your fat friend tonight, huh?" Trev jeered. "The freaky one with a backside like a horse."

"He's coming," I said. "And if he doesn't, one of his friends will."

"Danu, please, *run*!" pleaded Aunt Esme as she unsuccessfully tried to wiggle out of Benny's grip.

Joe's words echoed in my head. *"You can take them."*

I took a deep breath and remembered Mario's words on the last day of his class. *"Don't ever let them see if you are frightened. Explode and move."*

I took another deep breath. "HIYAAAAAAAAH!" I screamed as I leaped toward Trev, put my foot outside of and behind his leg, my palm up to his chin, pushed with all the force I could, and over he went. "Elbow, Aunt Esme," I called, as I ran and wrestled Benny from behind to let go of her. "Use your elbows."

Aunt Esme did exactly as she was told and delivered a few swift back jerks. I went for his eyes, and he quickly released her.

By this time, Trev was struggling back onto his

feet. I didn't give him time to recover and ran toward him, stepped between his legs, and kneed him squarely in the groin. "I hope you have an excellent career as a soprano," I said, as once again he toppled to the ground.

On seeing Trev writhing around in pain, Benny looked uncertain but soon regained his composure. "No one knees my friend," he growled as he ran toward me. But I was ready. I ran toward him with my arms raised, and he was so busy trying to figure out if I was going to punch him that he didn't notice that I'd put my right foot out, and over he went, landing in a heap on top of Trev.

"Come on!" I yelled to Aunt Esme, who suddenly seemed to be frozen in place. "Run."

I grabbed her hand and raced toward the apartment building and up the stairs. We flew into the apartment, quickly put the chain across the door, and double-locked all of the locks. Behind us, I could hear the sound of police sirens, while, at the same time, my phone rang in my pocket.

Aunt Esme slumped to the floor as I answered the phone.

"You okay?" asked Joe's voice.

As I was talking, I ran to the kitchen window to see if the boys were going to try and follow us. No chance. Down below was the wonderful sight of them being handcuffed and shoved into the back of a police car.

"Joe, why didn't you come?" I asked breathlessly.

"I called the cops instead," he said. "In case you needed backup. Sometimes you've got to make use of the facilities here on planet Earth. Did they get them?"

"They got them," I said. "Thanks." Behind me in the hall, I could hear the sound of Aunt Esme sobbing. "Better go, Joe. Aunt Esme needs me."

"Told you she did," he said and then hung up.

I went back into the hall and sank down next to Aunt Esme. "Hey, it's all right now. The police have got them."

I put my arm around her, but that only made her cry louder.

"Aunt Esme, what is it? We're safe now. What can I do?"

"N–N–Nothing . . ." she said and sniffed.

"Well, I can't leave you here on the floor. Come on, get up. Come into the living room."

She did as she was told and shuffled after me with the meekness of a little girl who had had a nightmare. I let her cry a little, and then she finally wiped her eyes and looked around the room. That made her start again.

"Uh-uh . . . uh-uh . . . *waaaaah* . . ."

"Oh, God," I said as I looked around. "You hate it, don't you? I'm sorry. I . . . I . . . suppose I should have waited . . ."

"No . . . No . . . (*sniff*) uh-uh . . . (*bigger sniff*) I . . .

I . . . l–l–love it. I *love* it. I love *all* of it."

"So why are you crying?"

"Because I'm so useless and have been terrible at taking care of you, and you've been unhappy, and it's my fault, and it's no wonder you want to leave, and no wonder no one ever comes here, and I don't have any friends and have to work all the time to pretend that I have a life when, really, I don't," Aunt Esme blurted out without stopping for a breath. "And I'm lonely and so glad that you're here so that I don't have to come back to an empty apartment anymore. All I ever wanted was a real home, but I am completely useless at it–even the plant I bought died because nobody or nothing wants to stay around me for long . . . uh-uh . . . buhuh . . . *waaaahhhh* . . ."

While she sat and cried like a baby, I scanned my mind for what to do. Call my dad? Call Joe? Make her some tea? In the end, I just held her hand and let her cry it out.

And then she began to laugh. And that was even more freaky deaky. I began to think that maybe she was cracking up completely, and I should call someone and get her carried off and locked up.

And then she hugged me.

"Danu. Do you think we could maybe start again. Me and you?"

* * *

Epilogue

Aunt Esme and I moved three months later.

It was a shame to leave our new fancy apartment, but we had outgrown the place and needed somewhere bigger–not only for entertaining the constant stream of visitors that always seemed to be around lately, but also so that Rosa could live with us. When Aunt Esme realized that Rosa had been sleeping on the sofa at her cousin's house, she invited her to come and live with us right away.

The most perfect house went up for sale only half a mile away from Osbury, and Aunt Esme leaped at the chance to own it and made an offer. At first we thought that it was going to be too expensive, but thanks to P.J.'s marvelous makeover on the apartment, we made a profit on the sale, which helped pay for the house. Of course, we hired P.J.'s services right away, and he made the house look wonderful. It has four bedrooms–one for me, one for Aunt Esme, one for Rosa, and one for Dad or my brother, if they ever come to visit.

The best part—it has a yard in the back with apples trees and a vegetable garden. My brother, Luke, has already stayed a few times. I think that he has a crush on Rosa, which is why we're seeing more of him. It's nice to see him, whatever his excuse is for being here. Joe and Mario are also regular visitors, and although my month as a Zodiac Girl is over, I still go to Mario's classes and Joe still passes on his favorite recipes. Rosa, Aunt Esme, and I have all become excellent cooks. My astrology book says that everything Jupiter touches expands. And that has certainly been true, including our waistlines!

Aunt Esme cut back her hours at the office and is much more relaxed and happy these days. In fact, we've become good friends. She still hasn't accepted the idea about the planets being here in human form, and I haven't pushed it with her. One thing at a time, and she does like Joe and Mario—and that's what is most important.

Best of all, we have a dog and a cat. Aunt Esme and I went to the Humane Society together and chose them. The dog is a red setter with gorgeous copper-colored hair. We called him Bluey. The cat is a black Persian with vivid orange eyes. We called her Honey. Like me and Aunt Esme, I think both of them are glad to have a home and space to run around after being cooped up in a cage.

At school, things couldn't be better. Nurse Torturer is extremely happy that I no longer have dreadlocks or hair extensions, because my hair grows quickly and I don't need them anymore. Joele, Chloe, and Sushila have adopted me as part of their group, and although I will never forget my friends back home, it does feel great to have friends to hang out with who live nearby and go to the same school as me. My grades are back up again, and next semester we're going on a school trip to Washington, D.C. I am going to write about it as the first of my "travel diaries."

Dad will be back for Christmas. Now that I have a real home, I don't mind so much that he's away–in fact, I think it will be nice for him to come back to somewhere welcoming and cozy.

And as for Trev and Benny, the police picked them up on the night that they tried to attack Aunt Esme. According to the local newspaper, the police found a whole pile of stolen goods at Trev's from recent break-ins, and now both of them are doing time.

Part of me feels sorry for them. They didn't need to have acted so stupid, but then they didn't have the amazing people to help them like I did when I was acting like a dingbat. At the beginning of the semester, it felt like my life was over, but now, it feels like it's just begun. I feel more like my old self.

The real Danu. Unafraid of the world and happy with my life. I was so unhappy when I was angry with everyone and everything.

At the end of the semester, when Mr. Beecham asked me to stand up in class and read my latest poem, this is how it went,

"My aunt is full of chocolate cake,
My guardian is a star,
The planets, they look over us
And home is not that far."

The Sagittarius Files

Characteristics, Facts, and Fun

November 22nd–December 21st

One of life's positive people–that's Sagittarius to a tee. They see the best in others, and they are always thoughtful and generous. They are good at seeing both sides of an argument . . . empathy could be their middle name. Their optimistic attitude is contagious.

However, being a fire sign means that they can be impatient and even self-destructive if things don't work out the way they want them to. They can be oversensitive sometimes . . . chilling out a little now and then would help them calm down.

Element:	Fire
Color:	Blue, purple, white
Birthstone:	Lapis lazuli
Animal:	Horse, dog
Lucky day:	Thursday
Planet:	Ruled by Jupiter

Sagittarius' best friends are likely to be:
Gemini
Aries
Leo
Sagittarius

Sagittarius' enemies are likely to be:
Scorpio
Pisces

A Sagittarius's idea of heaven would be:
Going on a safari.

A Sagittarius would go crazy if:
Someone kept proving them wrong all the time . . . it's their way, or the highway!

Famous Sagittariuses:
Christina Aguilera
Ludwig van Beethoven
Walt Disney
Katie Holmes
Ozzy Osborne
Brad Pitt
Britney Spears

Here's the first chapter of another fantastic **Zodiac Girls** story, **Discount Diva**.

Chapter One

The Crazy Maisies

I wish, I wish, I wish I could go, I thought when our homeroom teacher, Mrs. Creighton, first made the announcement.

". . . I will be taking names for the trip in the next week," she continued. "All those who want to go must register before the end of May, which only gives you one week."

A school trip to Venice. Two weeks in sunny Italy. I wanted to go more than anything, ever, since the beginning of eternity and even before that.

"You going to put your name down, Tori?" asked Georgie when the bell rang and we headed out of the classroom for our lunch break.

I shrugged my shoulders as if I didn't really care. "Maybe," I said.

"I definitely am," said Megan, catching up with us and linking arms. "Mom said I could go on the next school trip, wherever it was."

"Me, too," said Hannah, linking arms with Megan.

"Me, too," said Georgie. "Which means you have to come, Tori. It wouldn't be the same without you. The Crazy Maisies hit Europe."

Me, Hannah, Megan, and Georgie. We called ourselves the Crazy Maisies. My mom used to call me Crazy Maisy when I was little and acting silly. Me and my friends act silly a lot–hence the name.

"Venice isn't *that* great," I said. "Too many tourists. Florence is much more interesting." Ha. Like I'd been to either of them. Not. But I had heard my well-traveled aunt Phoebe saying that Venice was so full of tourists these days that you could hardly move.

"You *have* to come," said Hannah. "And so what if there are lots of tourists? We'll be four of them!"

"Yeah," said Georgie. "Italy, here we come!"

I felt a sinking feeling in my stomach. I was *so* going to miss out, but I could never tell them the real reason why I couldn't go.

"Si signora, pasta, cappuccino, tiramisu," I said, trying to remember all the Italian words that I had ever heard and to distract them from trying to persuade me to go. I'd have to think up some excuse that they'd all buy later.

"Linguine, Botticelli, spaghetti " Megan joined in.

"Da Vinci, Madonna, pizzeria, Roma," said Hannah.

Then they started singing a song that we'd done in music class last quarter. We'd had a substitute teacher who made us sing songs about different places around the world. "Trying to broaden your horizons," he said as he taught us folk songs from Italy to India. By the end of the quarter, however, I think he was glad to broaden his horizons and move on to another school where the students weren't tone-deaf.

"When the moon hits your eye like a big pizza pie, that's amore . . ." my friends chorused off-key and in terrible Italian accents.

A few ninth-grade girls sloped past and looked at us as if we were crazy. I play-acted that I wasn't with them, but Georgie dragged me back, and Hannah and Megan got down on their knees, put their hands on their hearts, and continued hollering away at the top of their lungs.

Crazy. They all are. And they'll have a great time in Venice, that's for sure. Another thing was for sure: no way would I be going with them. No way, José.

During lunch, we went out into the playground, found a bench on the sunny side, and did each other's hair. When we first met, only Georgie, out of the four of us, had long hair. After a short time hanging out together, we all decided to grow it to the same length so that we could play hairdresser, and long hair is best to experiment with. Georgie and Megan are blonde, although Megan's hair is thicker and golden blonde, while Georgie's is fine platinum blonde. Hannah and I have nomal brown hair, although Hannah has had chestnut highlights put in hers lately. It looks totally cool. I'd love to have highlights, but that's another thing to add to the "not going to happen unless my mom wins the lottery" list. I think Georgie's the prettiest of the four of us, although Megan and Hannah are good-looking in their own ways too. Hannah could pass for being Mexican. She has olive skin and amazing dark brown eyes that look enormous when she puts on makeup. Megan has a sweet face, bright blue eyes, and a tiny nose like a doll. Out of all of us, boys mostly pay attention to Georgie and me, though. Hannah and Megan say it's because I'm pretty too, but sometimes I wonder if the main reason that boys talk to me is to get to Georgie. I'm not big in the confidence department. Although somedays I can look okay, I could look a lot better if I got my hair done and bought some cool new clothes and makeup, but I doubt if that's going to happen anytime soon. Reason is, my family are broke and a half, so it's hard trying to keep up on the appearance front. Most of my clothes come from thrift stores, and I worry that my friends will find out. At school, girls who don't wear the latest designer duds get called

Discount Diva because their clothes don't have recognizable labels. Megan, Georgie, and Hannah have no idea that I'm Queen Discount Diva.

"I think we should go for a really sophisticated look when we're in Venice," said Megan as she pulled back Georgie's hair and began to braid it.

"No. I think we should wear it loose," said Hannah.

"Yeah," said Georgie. "Loose and romantic looking. There might be some cute Italian boys to flirt with."

Oh, no! Boys! Italian boys. I hadn't thought of that. What if one of my friends got a boyfriend and I wasn't there to share it all with her? What if all *three* of them got boyfriends and had their first kisses? It might happen. I've heard that Italy is a really romantic place. *Romeo and Juliet* happened over there, and they were way into each other. I've also heard that Italian boys are very hot-blooded. (I'm not totally sure what that means and whether they really do have hotter blood than us because they live in a warmer climate. Whatever.) Apparently, they are more forward than American boys, who mostly seem more interested in computers than they do in girls. Anyway, I would be left so far behind in the game of love. I'd be like Cinderella left at home while everyone else went to the ball. Eek! That would be so *tragic.* The Crazy Maisies did everything new together–that way we could talk about it all and see how we all felt.

"Ow," said Hannah with a wince as I brushed her hair up into a ponytail. "You're hurting me."

"Sorry," I said and made myself brush more gently. I didn't mean to take my frustration out on her, but all the talk for the next few weeks would be about the trip. And then they'd go, and I'd be on my own. And then they'd come back, and all the talk would be about the trip again. And I'd have nothing to say because I wouldn't have been there. I'd be left out. It would be awful. Luckily, Megan changed the subject and began making plans for the weekend. A new comedy movie was on at the local theater. Of course, everyone was up for seeing it.

"Cool!" said Georgie. "And we could go for snacks afterward?"

Megan and Hannah nodded enthusiastically. "Lots of those Mexican spicy cheesy taco thingies. I loooove them."

"Ice cream for me," said Georgie. "Pistachio with . . . strawberry."

"Pecan fudge is my favorite." I joined in.

"We'll have to do the early show, around six o'clock, or Mom won't be able to pick me up," said Hannah.

I did a quick calculation as they were discussing how they were going to get there and back and what they were going to eat. I'd need money for the movie. The bus. Snack. Coke . . . Nope. No way I could do it on my allowance money. I get around a fourth of what my friends get, and some weeks when things are really tight, Mom can't give us anything at all–us being me, my older sister, Andrea, and my two brothers, William and Daniel. I took a deep breath and got ready to apply my usual philosophy: *when the going gets tough, the tough bluff it.*

"I can't make it tonight. Mom got me and Dan and Will tickets for the Cyber Queens' gig."

"The Cyber Queens? Wow! You *lucky* thing!" said Georgie.

"You've kept quiet about that this week," said Megan. "Those tickets are like the hottest things around."

Hannah playfully punched my arm. "Yeah. Why didn't you tell us?"

"Mom only told us last night. It was a surprise for when we got home."

"A surprise? That's *so* awesome," said Georgie. "Your mom is so cool. I wish my mom did stuff like that. I bet my mom hasn't even heard of the Cyber Queens. Can she get the rest of us tickets?"

"Don't think so," I replied. "I think she got the last ones."

"Take your digital camera." said Hannah. "Take lots of pictures to show us."

"Sure," I said.

I felt guilty when the bell rang for our afternoon

classes. Not only did I not have tickets for the Cyber Queens, but I don't have a digital camera either, even though I'd told everyone that my grandma had gotten me one as an early birthday present. I lied. I don't really like doing it, but sometimes it's necessary. I have to make things up so that they don't think that I'm a total loser. My friends all have rich parents who buy them all the latest stuff: iPods, cell phones with cameras, computer games, designer clothes. And they've all got their own TVs and their own computers in their bedrooms. I don't even have my own bedroom. Not even my own bed. Not really. I have to share a room and a bunk bed with my sister, Andrea. Sometimes I sleep on the downstairs sofa just to get a little space, although even then I have to share it–with our cats, Molasses and Meatloaf (my brother Will named them. Molasses is black, and Meatloaf is a tabby.) Anyway, my friends would surely dump me if they knew the truth about my situation and how poor we really are compared to them.

When we first all started hanging out together as a group at the beginning of this year, to put them off coming over, I told them that our house was being rehabbed from top to bottom–kitchen, bathroom, the whole thing. I keep telling the girls that it's been a "nightmare" with the workers who keep letting us down. It's an expression I've heard their parents use a million times. So far, they haven't been over a lot, but when they have, my excuses have worked, because the fact is, our house *does* look like it's in the middle of being rehabbed. The walls are patchy, with daubs of paint here and there where one of us decided to try out some paint samples, but there wasn't enough money to buy the paint. There are no carpets on the stairs. The carpets that are on the floor are worn. There are floorboards up here and there. The whole place looks like it needs to be ripped out and redone from top to toe, so my story has never met with any questions. Sometimes I think that Georgie may have caught on, but she's never come out and said anything–not yet, anyway. It can be stressful on the rare occasions when the girls do come over, though, as I'm afraid that Andrea, Will, or Dan might blow my cover. Instead, I try and make sure that we hang out at Megan, Hannah, or Georgie's houses. I say, oh, the floor's up again, or the scaffolding is dangerous, or the water's off or something. They're so sympathetic that I feel rotten sometimes, especially because Georgie seems to like coming to our house, and she always brings something with her like some yummy muffins or cookies or pineapple juice (my favorite) or something.

All of my friends are kind. They invite me to sleep over at their houses when I lay on the rehab nightmare scenario really thick–like, last week, I said that a plumber had burst a pipe and there was water everywhere. I like going to Georgie's place the best. It's awesome. They have five bedrooms at her house for just her and her mom. Five. And seeing as Georgie is an only child, that means that they have three spare rooms. Three. I wish I could go and live with her sometimes, although I know deep down that I'd miss my family and especially the cats. Her house is like a palace compared to where I live. I feel like a princess when I'm there, and her mom never interferes with her life. Not like my house. No privacy there. Not even in the bathroom since there is always someone knocking on the door telling whoever is in there to hurry up.

Some days, like today, being poor stinks. It was Friday. May 12th. The whole world would be out enjoying the early summer sun this evening. Certainly half of our school would be. Everyone would be at the movies hanging out. Some of the older girls from our school would also be there, showing off the cool new outfits that they'd just bought. There would probably even be some boys there from Marborough High School down the road. And I'll have to miss out on the whole outing because I haven't got enough money to go.

As we got up to go back into school, there was a

sudden blast of wind that blew up dust and debris from the playground.

"Whoa," said Georgie as her skirt billowed up. "Where's that come from?"

"Dunno," said Meg, "but let's run."

In an instant, more papers and candy wrappers began to blow in a mini tornado around the playground as the students headed back inside. A piece of paper flew toward me and stuck to my hand. I flicked it off, but it fluttered back again, and we all laughed, because after I brushed it off for the second time, it seemed to follow me as we headed for the door back into the school. It was dancing along behind me, and just before I reached the door, it blew right up, until it covered my face so that I couldn't see.

"Bleurgh," I blustered as I pulled it away from my eyes.

"Maybe it's meant for you," said Megan, taking the paper away from me. "Let's see what it is."

"Yeah, right," I said. "Maybe it's a message from a fairy." I was teasing her, because last year, she was into fairies and angels, and her bedroom was covered with posters of them.

"What does it say?" asked Hannah.

Megan scanned the paper. "Dear Tori. You are to go to the secret fairy hideout at midnight on Friday night . . ."

I punched her arm playfully. I knew she was making

that up. "What does it really say?"

"It looks like some sort of promotion-type thing," she replied. "Um . . . advertising local businesses kind of thing. A beauty salon in Osbury. A café/deli. An astrology website. Stuff like that."

"I'll chuck it," I said and took it to put it in the garbage can in the corner of the playground. As I threw it away, there was a flash of lightening and then a rumble of thunder in the distance. I glanced up. The sky had darkened, threatening sudden rain, so I raced back to join the others at the door.

"The fairies are angry that you threw away their business card," joked Georgie.

"Yeah, right. Fairies and elves are alive and well and have taken over Osbury." I laughed back.

Seconds later, the skies opened, and rain pelted down, so we darted inside as quick as we could.

"Phew," I said as we raced down the corridor. "Just in time."

As we settled into class, our teacher, Miss Wilkins, was busy shutting the windows that had been open earlier in the morning. The rain continued pouring down, and the wind was still whipping up debris outside. As she reached the last window at the back of the classroom near my desk, a piece of paper blew inside. It sailed right across the classroom and landed right in front of me.

Megan, Hannah, and Georgie turned to look. I glanced down. It was the same piece of paper that had been following me in the playground! Beauty salon, deli, astrology website . . .

Maybe Megan was right and there were fairies and guardian angels out there. Maybe this was a message from one of them in code or something. *Yeah. And I'm the richest girl in the world,* I thought. However, the paper arriving in front of me *did* make me wonder. I didn't believe in a fairyland like Megan, but I *did* believe that some things are meant to be. Like fate. Or destiny. And this *was* a coincidence. I couldn't deny that. Maybe it *was* meant for me. I was about to put the paper in my backpack to look at more carefully later when Miss Wilkins closed the last window and turned back to the class. As she did, she saw the paper that had landed on my desk.

"That litter is blowing everywhere!" she said as she picked it up, ripped it into tiny pieces, and took it to the front where she threw it away. "Such a nuisance."

Oh, no, I thought as I watched her do it. *There goes the message about my destiny–straight into the trash!*